Pacer

Being a real reporter would change my life. Every kid in Sagamon High School reads *The Sentinel*. My name would be as well known as Barbara Walters's. Liz Ray would probably pop over to my lunch table to tell me what the Hi Gals were doing. It wouldn't be as good as belonging, but a heck of a lot better than being completely out of it. Maybe something hysterical would happen in the locker room, and Beeb would stop me in the hall and say, "How about this for your column . . .?" They'd ask me to all their parties so their names'd get in the paper.

LOU WILLETT STANEK was born on a farm in the small town of Vandalia, Illinois. She now lives in New York City.

Megan's Beat

Lou Willett Stanek

Pacer BOOKS FOR YOUNG ADULTS

BERKLEY BOOKS, NEW YORK

This Berkley/Pacer book contains the complete
text of the original hardcover edition.

MEGAN'S BEAT

A Berkley/Pacer Book, published by arrangement
with E.P. Dutton, Inc.

PRINTING HISTORY
E.P. Dutton edition / 1983
Berkley/Pacer edition / September 1985

ISBN: 0-425-08416-7
RL: 5.6

Pacer is a trademark belonging to
The Putnam Publishing Group.

A BERKLEY BOOK ® TM 757,375
Berkley/Pacer Books are published by The Berkley Publishing Group,
200 Madison Avenue, New York, New York 10016.
The name "BERKLEY" and the stylized "B" with design
are trademarks belonging to Berkley Publishing Corporation.
PRINTED IN THE UNITED STATES OF AMERICA

To Dannon, W.G.N.

One

* * * * * * * * * * * * *

Going to high school in town has been just about all I could think about for the last couple of years, and today I really was going to go. I knew I had left the house too early, but I sure didn't want to miss the bus the first day. Daddy was plowing the twenty acres across the road from where the bus would pick me up, and he had already made three rounds since I'd been standing here about ready to blow up from excitement.

I'd been planning this day since the first time Mother and I went into Kramer's Drug Store for a soda after we'd done the grocery shopping. This girl named Liz Ray, she's Judge Ray's daughter and *everybody* knows who they are, came in with all of her friends. She has long hair so light, it's almost white, like moonlight, and you could just tell she was the most popular girl in the group. The first time I saw them, Liz and two other girls had junior high cheerleading outfits on, and they were all excited about a game they had just won. I guess I really was staring at them because Mother said, "Just think, Megan, in a couple of years you'll be sitting over there giggling with them about boys and games." I'd been dreaming about them being my friends ever since. Especially Liz.

I went out in the middle of the road to see if the bus was in sight, and I saw it stop at Tom's. He's my best friend. He's a boy, and he's my friend, but he's not my boyfriend, if you know what I mean. His farm borders ours, and the Arnolds have known my folks forever. In the summer the two families get together, and we crank up the old wooden freezer to make fresh peach ice cream, and in the fall we get together during hunting season for a quail fry—things like that. All the girls at Heckathorne Elementary School thought Tom was terrific, but he seems like a brother to me. They don't know the trouble I've had with him.

Sometimes Tom doesn't have any more backbone than a banana. His dark hair's real curly, and he's got a ton of freckles. I swear he's as short as a midget now, even though we used to be about the same size. Tom and I fight each other all the time, but at Heckathorne we'd take on the whole group if they ganged up on either one of us. On the eighth grade baseball team he was catcher, and I pitched. Sometimes he almost killed me when he threw the ball back so hard. On purpose.

I was glad he was going to be around at Sagamon High School. I wasn't worried or anything, but it always takes a while to get the hang of something new. I sure never had any trouble at Heckathorne. I don't mean to brag or anything, but those kids kind of depended on me to keep things moving. Of course, there were only thirty-five of us in the whole school, but I even helped Mr. Ehlers with teaching first- and second-grade reading classes. I never could understand why some of those little kids had so much trouble catching on to reading. I knew how to do that before I even got to school.

The bus made an incredible racket and kicked up a lot of dust, but I was too excited to worry about it. Henry's been driving one of the five school buses that takes farm kids in to high school for about a hundred years, and he thinks he's a comedian. "Well, if it ain't Joe Morgan's black-eyed little boy," he said when he threw open the door for me to jump on.

"Gee, thanks a lot, Henry! Just what I need to make me feel good on my first day." I knew he was talking about my figure. I have to buy boy's jeans because I'm not rounded enough to fill the ones designed with a girl's curves in mind. I might as well wear boy's sweaters, too, if you want to know the truth, but I had more important things than that to worry about today.

"Hey, Megan, you scared?" Betty Sue yelled from the back.

"Megan's ain't scared of nothin', are you?" Dick Krug said, and punched me on the shoulder. Tim Gable was sitting with Dick, and he just waved. Tim's kind of quiet.

"'Course I'm not scared," I said, and almost fell on

3

my nose when Henry took off with a lurch. "All you guys remember to bring those programs they mailed us?"

"Will you sit down," Tom said, and pulled on my belt till I fell into the seat next to him. Chaos and excitement carried us into town.

When we finally got to school, everything was so disorganized at first, I thought I was in a madhouse, but eventually they herded us all into the gym for a freshman assembly. Right then I got this awful feeling that riding the bus would be the pits. None of us bus kids knew where to sit, and everybody kind of bunched up and kept stumbling into each other like a herd of cows in a pen. I saw Liz Ray and her gang prance down to the front row and wave to the upperclassmen who were on the stage, so I grabbed Tom's arm and marched us right down behind them. He went, but if his mother ever heard what he said to me all during that assembly, she'd crucify him. Betty Sue, Tim, Dick, and those kids all hugged the back wall. I bet no one even noticed Betty Sue, and she's kind of flashy. Wears too much jewelry and stuff.

The president of the student council told us what clubs and teams and things we could try out for. He kept saying things like, "I know Pris White won't be interested in this, but the Thespian Club will do a freshman play this year." She was a friend of Liz Ray's, and they all looked at her and gave her a thumbs-up sign. You just knew she already had the lead before anybody else even tried out.

4

I was just getting sicker and sicker. Everything he mentioned met after school. I punched Tom and whispered, "Will the bus wait for us if we sign up for some of these clubs?"

"Of course not, dummy!" Tom hissed back at me.

Some girl sitting next to Liz Ray turned around and said, "Shhh."

"What's your problem, Jane?" Liz said.

"Those stupid farm kids are making so much racket I can't hear."

I felt as if she'd knocked the breath out of me. I whipped around to see how Tom was taking it, but he was looking at his shoes and didn't meet my eyes. I would have liked to sock her. But just then the president said something that made me feel better. The school newspaper staff was chosen by the sample articles students turned in. If your article was chosen, you were automatically on the staff.

I threw up my hand to ask a question, and Tom mouthed, "Megan, will you keep quiet."

"Yes? The girl with the black braid in the fourth row," said the president, pointing at me.

"When does the staff meet?" I asked.

"The editorial staff, which is made up of juniors and seniors, meets Thursday morning before school, but they just post assignments for the reporters."

Great! I could write the pieces at home, and the newspaper was better than any club. I'd always had these big dreams about being a reporter on a newspaper like *The Chicago Tribune*. I want to be one of those journalists who rides around in a jeep covering revolutions and stuff. I'll probably have my own jeep and carry a camera over my shoulder. Right while the battle's going on. I'll duck under the crossfire and record what's happening: *This is Megan Morgan reporting from the scene of the action. Whoops, that one came close. Even though journalists have been ordered back behind the lines, I've been able to double back to give you an eyewitness account....*

"Now I want to introduce the varsity basketball players because we expect all of you freshmen to come out to back the dynamite team Sagamon's going to have this year," the president was saying.

Tom poked me in the ribs and pointed to Beeb Barber. I blushed and grabbed his finger. Last year our fathers had brought us in to a few Saturday night games, and I'd made the dumb mistake of telling Tom how I thought Beeb was the best-looking guy in Sagamon County.

Beeb must be six feet tall, and he's only a sophomore. Even a string bean like me could wear heels to a school dance with him. Fat chance that will ever happen, of course. He played varsity when he was a freshman. One of the lights from the stage was shining on his hair, and I thought I'd just die. It's the color of an old brick with just a lightning streak of gold in front. Even from where Tom and I was sitting I could see that his eyes were the color of chocolate, rich chocolate. I had cut his picture out of the sports page last year, but it was a tiny little thing and kind of blurred.

When the president called Beeb's name, I thought Pris White was going to have a fit. She kept jumping out of her seat and clapping like a crazy woman. Her arm hit Liz Ray's books, and they went skittering across the floor, but by then Mike Brooks, another varsity player, was being introduced, and Liz jumped up and screamed for him. She and Pris were hugging each other and jumping up and down all over Liz's stuff. It looked as if Mike Brooks was Liz's boyfriend, and Pris White was probably going with Beeb. I felt just as if all the stuffing were coming out of me. Nothing was the way I'd dreamed it would be. I slumped over.

"Megan, what's the matter with you now?" Tom whispered real softly, and then glanced up to see if that girl Jane in the front row was going to yell at us again.

"I feel like a little mouse," I said, and was glad the bell rang so we could get out of there and go to our classes. Tom and I both had biology first period. We had a hard time finding Room 132, but when we were finally headed in the right direction, I started thinking about the newspaper staff again.

"The president said anyone who wanted to write for the paper would have to have an article submitted by Friday." I sighed. "Now how will I know enough about this place to write anything that soon?"

"You could write about how it feels to be Megan

the Mouse," Tom said, and then about had convulsions, he laughed so hard. He can be gross.

Our teacher's name was Mrs. Horner, and she had to fill out a lot of papers and stuff, so I started doodling in the back of my notebook. Liz Ray, Jane, and Pris White were in our class, and I was trying to hear what they were saying, but I didn't want them to see me watching them—not that they were paying the least bit of attention.

I drew a mouse with a sad little face, and then I put a cartoon balloon over his head that said, "I'm afraid all of those kids are going to trample me to death." I passed it across the aisle to Tom, and he wrote, "I don't even know where the john is." With my red pen I added a beanie with a big F for freshman, and the silly mouse looked even more forlorn.

Since there wasn't anything else to do at lunch and none of the other kids so much as looked at us, we kept adding silly things for the mouse to say.

When I got home that night, I really didn't even want to think about how awful the day had been. I went up to my room after supper and started writing a story as if I were that mouse and was looking at Sagamon High School from his point of view. My little sister, Lizzie, thought it was funny, but five-year-olds will laugh at anything.

And school didn't improve one bit. Although when you added up all the bus kids, there were more of us than kids from town, they didn't even know we were there. They just ignored us and kept on having a super time laughing and talking and running the whole school. We were just lumps to be maneuvered around when they wanted to get to each other in the crowded halls.

The only good thing that happened was because of my mouse story. About a week later my homeroom teacher handed it to me with a note attached that said:

Congratulations. We liked your story, and if you could add 50 words, we would like to publish it in the first issue of The Scoop. *We have selected three freshman reporters, and your assignments will be posted on the bulletin board outside the student activity office three weeks before we go to press. If you have any questions, please stop into the office. We will hold a joint "get acquainted" staff meeting later on this month.*

The Editors

Fifty words? I'd write five thousand standing on my head if they wanted me to. The note was the first thing that made me feel as if I were even a student in this place.

The very next morning I added fifty words to my article and put it in my notebook. I could hardly wait to hand it in.

Just my luck. Beeb Barber and Mike Brooks *would* have to be walking down the sidewalk just as the stupid school bus clanged to a stop in front of the school. It happens almost every morning.

I let my history notebook slip out of my hand and

clatter to the floor. While Henry watched everyone else push their way out, I bent down, pretending to collect my papers. Sometimes you just have to take charge of your own fate because it seems as if there's some screwball in charge of it.

My hair's black and thick, and, of course, it swung like a heavy rope, sweeping up the filthy floor. Even though I'd almost broken my arm brushing it that morning, I'd rather have washed it again that night than have Beeb see me on the bus. He probably wouldn't even notice, actually. Mother thinks I'm pretty, but then mothers always do. She says my dark hair, eyes, and skin make me stand out. Makes me feel more like a blackout. I was in Beeb's English class, and as far as I could tell he d never even noticed I was there. I felt weird in that class with all those sopho-mores, anyway, even if it was supposed to be an honor to have been placed out of freshman English.

Well, I just can't let this place spook me, I decided while I was stalling around waiting for Beeb and Mike to go inside. I've just got to get it figured out. But in the meantime there's no reason to advertise that I'm being hauled to school like stock going to market.

Henry turned sideways in the driver's seat and grinned at me like he knew I was hiding.

''You goin' in there to get yourself smartened up, Megan, or should I turn this ole jalopy around and run you back out to that hayfield Joe was attackin' this mornin'?''

"I know all I need to know about hayfields, Henry, so I guess I might as well get along in there. Dropped my history notes. I guess I've got them all now."

"Too bad your dad ain't got a boy who'd take an interest in hayfields. Joe Morgan's spread's the best in the county, I always say."

Henry thinks I should be thankful to be a Morgan just because my dad owns a lot of land, is president of the Farmers Association, and stuff like that. I like my dad okay, and my mother's terrific, but even though I tell them every night, they can't seem to understand what it's like to be a virtual prisoner seven miles away from everything that's going on. And it would be one year, nine months, and fourteen days before I'd get my driver's license. Dumb system. I'd been driving a tractor since I was ten.

My watch said I had six minutes to get to my locker and pick up my book for biology. I'd better scoot, I thought as I got off the bus and waved to Henry.

I went tearing into biology like a madwoman and almost died when I hit Jane Day on the shoulder and sent her spinning against the wall. She'd been standing just inside the door, talking to Liz Ray, of all people. They looked startled, and I flushed. I felt as if I had about as much grace as our old cow, Harmony.

"Coach's looking for a good back, Megan. Maybe you better try out," Liz said, but she smiled and didn't sound mean.

I knew they had probably been talking about Hi

Gals, this neat club Liz and her friends had started. You couldn't go to Sagamon without knowing about the Hi Gals. You got to be one by invitation only. My stomach clutched. I have to admit that when someone's doing something I think is neat and I'm not included, it really tears me up. Daddy says I'm like a bulldog who won't let go of a bone, but he just never seems to know how hard I want for things. I knew I'd be a terrific Hi Gal. Even after class started, I couldn't stop thinking about it because this being excluded was a new experience for me. I must have been staring out the window, because the next thing I knew the teacher was yelling at me.

"Megan? Megan Morgan! If I can interrupt your dreams long enough, I thought perhaps you might demonstrate to the class how to dissect this earthworm. A farm girl like you shouldn't be squeamish." Mrs. Horner held a wiggling, cigarlike worm with the tips of her fingers as if she didn't think the slimy thing was all that great herself.

Everybody snickered. Mrs. Horner's the kind of woman who'd tell a hunchback his jacket fits poorly. I heard someone up in the front row say "Hayseed," but I didn't give them the pleasure of knowing I'd heard. Actually I didn't even want to know who had said it. For over two weeks I'd kept my chin up by pure force of will. I knew it was going to quiver if I looked at another unfriendly face, and I had too much pride to let these kids know they were getting to me.

Two

* * * * * * * * * * * * * *

Tim Gable and Dick Krug sat behind me on the bus
going home. Dick kept putting this stupid rubber
snake down the collar of my shirt and saying, "What's
the matter, Megan? A farm girl shouldn't be squeamish." Betty Sue giggled as if he were really a comedian.

I told Dick I hoped he flunked biology so he could
spend two years learning how to be as mean and
cruel as Mrs. Horner. He was driving me crazier than
usual because I had other things to worry about. I'd
been thinking of asking to go to one of those boarding schools. I read a book once about a girl in Eng-
land who did that, but then she had hated the place.
Besides, Daddy'd be about as apt to send me to the
funny farm as to a boarding school. The other idea
I'd had was going to live with my aunt in town, just
till I grew up. I bet if Mother and Daddy knew what
I went through every day, they'd let me do it. Like
I was sitting on the floor outside my history class yesterday, reading the boring assignment one more time
before class started, and this senior boy came along
and jumped right over my head without even saying
"Boo." Unless they know you, they don't see you.

He could have kicked my brains out and just kept on going. Instead of this being the most exciting time of my life, I felt as if I'd moved to a foreign country that wasn't even an ally. My folks just had to understand.

Long before Henry stopped the bus in front of our lane, I could see Daddy with his pitchfork. He was standing on top of the stack. Bill Arnold, Tom's dad, was pitching bales of hay up to him, but he seemed to be more interested in watching the road. He kept shading his eyes and looking toward town.

Normally I would have gone over to ask to drive the truck that picked up the hay bales, but I knew tonight I better get up to the house to help Mother. When the neighbors pitch in to help with haying, they always stay for a big meal after they finish. Hay has to dry before you stack it, so they start after the sun dries the dew and stay through till supper. It's a feast—always two or three kinds of pie, usually ham and fried chicken both. The women around here kind of compete to see who can set out the best spread.

Our house is a big two-story white frame with a porch wrapped around the south and west sides. The corner is curved and covered with a trellis that holds up a clematis vine that looks like a big purple balloon of blossoms in the summer. Mother encourages the morning glories to climb around too. Daddy says morning glories are weeds, but Mother says weeds are just plants people haven't been smart enough to find a use for yet. She likes to liven things up with a splash of color. Her mother was French. "Flashy barbarians," Daddy says whenever Mother does something he thinks is outrageous. Which is often.

The house sits a quarter of a mile off the road, down a lane that's a lot like a roller coaster. The road dips down to a wooden bridge across a creek and then bumps up again. The house, barns, sheds, and all that stuff are on top of a hill, surrounded on three sides by ten acres of pasture that I really like. Cedar trees are sprinkled around the creek and a split-rail fence fitted together in a zigzag fashion borders it. The fence is older than Methuselah. When I was little, Mother used to play cowboys with me. The fence was our horses. Before I started high school, I used to think our farm was kind of pretty.

When the bus pulled away, I started running down the lane, but Daddy yelled at me from the hayfield. He came over to meet me.

"Megan, did you pass your mother on the way from town?" He sounded worried.

"No. What's she doing in town when she has men for supper?" I asked, and immediately wished I hadn't.

"Thought she had to have some fancy fresh meat. Our own chickens not good enough for her. She must've had trouble . . . maybe a wreck. Always did drive too fast. She should have been back two, three hours ago."

"Lizzie with her?"

"No. And that's another thing. The women in this

family are going to drive me to boozing. Lizzie was riding in the truck and didn't want to go with your mother, but she got tired of that and went up to the house. Came back with one of those little pigs squealing to beat thunder. She had a blue ribbon tied around his neck. Said she gave him a bubble bath in our tub! Probably kill the pig. Where *is* your mother?"

I was laughing so hard, I didn't hear the car, but Daddy did. Mother was driving too fast, as usual, but she had pulled over by the time we got up to the road. She was crying, and Daddy turned white as a ghost.

"Lucy, darlin', what happened? Are you hurt?"

Daddy reached into the car, touching her shoulder and cheek with his sweaty, dirty hands, but she just kept crying.

"Oh, Joe, I saw the most wonderful movie. They took Meryl Streep's child away from her and . . ."

I really thought he was going to kill her this time. I think she did too. She stopped crying real quick and started talking kind of breathless like.

"The movie was closing today, and I thought those men probably are tired of all that heavy food, and I went to that new deli in town and got all this lovely stuff . . . smoked turkey, goat cheese—"

"Cold food for men who've been pitching hay all day? Cheese made out of goat's milk? Lucy, sometimes I just don't know. . . ."

"Your father always said I'd never make a farmer's wife. Maybe you should have listened to him, Joe."

Mother sounded sad. I knew she was sorry to have upset Daddy. I also knew how she felt. We both had a way of doing things that seemed like good ideas until we saw how he looked at them. Then they just seemed silly.

Bill Arnold stayed for supper. When the rest of the men saw how angry Daddy was, they just sort of slunk away. Didn't relish sitting through a row at supper after working hard all day, I guess.

Bill was trying to wash the hayseed off out at the pump. It was getting dark, but I sat down on the well curb to wait for him. I could hear Mother banging things around on the stove and yelling at Lizzie about the pig.

"How's high school goin', Megan?" Bill asked while he rubbed the back of his neck with a red handkerchief.

"Awful! Bill, did you ever hear of the *Robert E. Lee?*"

"No. Can't stay that I have. Is that somethin' they've got up to the high school?"

"No. It's in St. Louis. You see, these Hi Gals— that's a club for the popular girls. They wear army jackets with their nicknames on the back and all hang out together. Well, last week I kept hearing them saying *Robert E. Lee, Robert E. Lee,* about ten thousand times a day and acting real excited until I thought I'd go bonkers. Finally I started into biology class, and three of them were talking about it, but when I came along, they stopped like I was a Russian spy planning on ruining Robert E. Lee's memory or something."

I put my head in my hands. I was glad it was dark. Now I was sorry I'd even told Bill. " 'Well,' I said to them, 'You don't have to stop, I know who he was.' I wish you could have heard how they laughed. This girl, Liz Ray, she shrieked, *'He?'* and then just fell into her friend Pris's arms and laughed like a baboon."

"I don't see nothing so funny about that, do you?" Bill said.

"Well, this teacher, Mrs. Horner, was watching, and she walked over to my desk and said real quietly, 'Megan, the *Robert E. Lee* is a big pleasure boat that goes up and down the river.' Then she went on writing the assignment on the board. I kind of whispered 'thanks.' I know she meant well, but I was mortified if you want to know the truth, and you don't like to be beholden to a teacher, you know?"

"No, I reckon you don't."

"I wish you guys had taken me and Tom for a ride on that thing before we started to high school." I looked toward the house and we both heard Mother and Daddy going at it again. "I guess I'll never get married, Bill."

"Then some man will be denied a lot of pleasure, Megan. You're like your mom. You've got a lot of drive," he said as he threw another handful of water on his face, so I couldn't see if he was laughing. I didn't expect anyone to be passing out compliments about Mother that night.

"When Ethel and I was first married, she used to do funny things now and then. You know, silly things." He sat down beside me but didn't seem to remember I was there. "Once I remember she put green food coloring in the gravy. I just had a fit. Asked her if she was trying to poison me. Food coloring don't have no taste. Don't know why I made such a fuss. She don't ever do anything ridiculous anymore. Sometimes I kind of wish she did."

We had scrambled eggs and bacon for supper. Daddy said Mother could put the goat cheese in the slop for the hogs as far as he was concerned.

Everyone was so gloomy, I should have known it was a crummy time to bring up my problems, but I thought maybe they would welcome a diversion, and with Bill there Daddy might try to be more reasonable. Besides, I was feeling desperate, and I'd been working on a plan for days.

"Daddy, riding that bus to school is just not working out. I think I'll have to get a room in town until I'm old enough to drive." I knew Daddy would hit the ceiling when he heard that. What I was working toward was a compromise. "I'll never learn a thing this way, never being there after school to see what's going on."

"Movin' to a boardin' house at thirteen? Now that's a crackerjack of an idea, kid," Daddy said, with more sarcasm than was called for.

"Maybe Aunt Betty would let you stay with her a few nights, Megan, when something important is happening," my mother said, just as I hoped she would. I knew it usually works better for her to bring up an idea than for me to suggest it to Daddy myself. But that just seemed to be the last straw for him. My timing was terrible. After what Mother had done this afternoon, he wasn't about to listen to her. You would have thought we were suggesting I move to Mars or somewhere.

"When I can't provide a roof over my children's heads and have to start farming them out to my sister, that's when I quit!"

"Why don't you just keep me home plowing then? I could be about as involved in things at school from the seat of that ole Allis as I could having to travel seven miles both ways."

"Megan, it'll do you good not to be running things for a change. Bill Ehlers spoiled you over at Hecka-thorne. The view from the back row won't hurt you at all for a while."

"Daddy, you've just got to understand that one of these days I'll have to be moving on."

"Plannin' on goin' far?"

"Far as I can, but right now I'll settle for just getting into town." If he'd heard them laugh at me in biology today, I bet he'd have let me go, I thought, but didn't say. It's not easy to admit, even to your father, that someone has made fun of you.

"You better stick around with us, Megan. We're so used to you tellin' us what to do, what would we do without your bossin'?"

Mother tried again. "Now, Joe. I bet Betty'd probably be glad to have her once in a while."

"Lucy, no wonder our kids do such nutty things. Your ideas are as crazy as theirs. When are you going to grow up?" Daddy looked at her with that I-don't-believe-it expression he often gets.

Bill Arnold and I exchanged knowing smiles, but Lizzie slipped out of her chair and crawled under the table. She sat there like a miniature curly-headed buddha with her hands over her ears and refused to come out until everybody stopped arguing. She even softened up Daddy. Everybody says she looks just like him, and he likes that. Probably when she goes to high school, he'll sell the farm and buy a house on Elm Street right next door to Liz Ray. Just when it's too late for us to be friends, of course.

I started upstairs to my room, and Bill said he better get on home to see how Tom was getting along. He had strained a muscle trying to lift a calf over a stanchion in the barn and slicktalked Ethel into letting him stay home from school so he could keep a heating pad on it.

We'd been in 4-H since we were kids, and Tom always raises a calf. He spends more time on those calves than normal boys do on their girl friends. When we joined that 4-H chapter, it might as well have been a knitting club. I sure wasn't going to waste my time if we didn't enter competitions. Now Tom's so set on raising a grand champion, you'd think competing had been his idea. At the time he wouldn't even help me convince our sponsors. Since I started high school I'm not so interested in 4-H anymore. Tom and Betty Sue might think it was neat, but I'd rather be a Hi Gal or a cheerleader now. I threw myself across my bed in disgust.

Frankly I think cows are boring, boring, boring. My horse, Prince, is my project. I trick ride him in competition. Every year I have to teach him some new ones. When I leave, I'll probably take Prince with me so I won't be homesick. I can keep Prince in a stable and ride him in the park when I get to be a big city reporter, but I'd look pretty silly walking down a fancy street with a calf on a leash.

I bet the kids in town would think 4-H is dumb. I wonder what they do with their spare time, other than go to Kramer's Drug Store for a Coke *after* that stupid bus leaves. And Mother thought I'd get to go with 'em. Boy, did she have a lot to learn!

Sometimes I try to imagine Beeb Barber outside of school, but my mind just blanks. I always see him in his crimson letter sweater walking around the halls with Mike Brooks, as confident as two kings. I try not to imagine him with Pris White. But Tom said he saw them with Liz and Mike at the movies one

Sunday afternoon. I hope I never do. I couldn't bear it!

I guess anybody would look good in a letter sweater, but that color just makes Beeb look regal. His dark red hair waves just enough . . . not in corkscrews like Tom's, but nice and easy. His shoulders must be a mile wide, and his hips are really narrow. It's just the way an athlete should look. His jeans fit him like they were tailored, and he smiles a lot. If I could wear his letter sweater, I'd throw away every top I own. I bet he doesn't give a hoot about cows. Why can't I make Daddy understand what I'm missing!

I flipped over on my back and stared up at the ceiling. I could see me and Beeb on that ceiling. What a team we would make. Me, editor of the paper, him, captain of the team. Probably they'd nominate us for class offices. I'd be president because I can make good speeches. Everybody would invite us to parties and stuff. We'd try to work 'em in. We wouldn't want to hurt anyone's feelings, of course. I'd have to have a ton of clothes.

Mother interrupted my dreams and made me come back down and help her load the dishwasher. Daddy read Lizzie her favorite story about a little pink pig. That kid's got a thing about pigs. When I started to complain about the dishes, Mother whispered, "Don't complain. Think how bad it would have been if we'd had all those men for supper."

We giggled.

When they went upstairs to bed, I guess Daddy had forgiven Mother, because they walked up arm in arm. Usually I feel a little embarrassed when they behave like that, even though when I get married I want my husband to be madly in love with me. But tonight I felt shut out and mad as anything. Daddy *always* forgave Mother finally, but I don't think he paid much attention to what she said about how I could stay with Aunt Betty. I don't know why he couldn't really listen to my problems sometimes. I couldn't go on like this. Something good just had to happen for me soon!

Three

* * * * * * * * * * * * * *

Something did happen! Something almost too good to believe, but it took a little time. I had begun to feel as if I really *were* that mouse in my story.

English class had quickly become the best and the worst part of my life. I loved to read the stories and write the essays Mr. Wills assigned, but since I was the only freshman in the class with all those sophomores, I felt a little funny expressing my opinion or sharing my work. They kept referring to what had happened last year in English class, what they'd read and everything, and of course I didn't have a clue to what they were talking about. Since this was the only class I had with any of them, I didn't really know a soul to ask, and it didn't seem like they were very interested in me.

Beeb Barber sat two rows across from me, but as far as he was concerned I might as well have been in Siam. Mr. Wills arranged us alphabetically, so Beeb sat in the second seat between Bud Adams and Mike Brooks. They were all buddies and horsed around before class. Mike and Bud did anyway. They were lunatics. Beeb was quieter, but he was tight with them. All I could do was watch and pretend I wasn't.

The day my miracle happened, Mr. Wills had been talking about F. Scott Fitzgerald's phrase, "It's always three o'clock in the morning in my soul." Wow, did I ever understand that! Right in the middle of our discussion someone knocked on the door. That hardly ever happened, so we all tried to see who Mr. Wills was talking to out in the hall, but he closed the door. When he stepped back in and said, "Megan, would you come out here, please," a hush fell over the room, but my heart was drumming a loud solo.

Horrible thoughts started running through my head: That mean ole sow Bertha had eaten up Lizzie. Daddy got his arm chewed off in the cornpicker. The gypsies carried off our chickens . . . and Mother. Daddy had told her over and over again, not to let them on the place.

I was scared to death. I dragged my lead legs to the door. Twenty-five pair of eyes watched me march bravely toward tragedy. Beeb Barber finally had noticed me.

Mr. Wills was young and cocky as a banty rooster. It was his first year teaching, and he was a little too sarcastic for my taste. He knew a lot about English, but he didn't know much about Sagamon. As soon as we were in the hall, he introduced me to John Finley, the editor of *The Sagamon Sentinel,* as if I didn't know the man whose Democratic editorials had been making my father's blood boil for twenty-five years.

A buzz and then a roar sounded off in the classroom, so Mr. Wills scurried back in there and left me staring at John Finley with my mouth hanging open like an idiot. What could he possibly want with me?

"Megan, as you probably know, we print *The Scoop* down at the *Sentinel* office. I always look at the galleys before we go to press, and I really liked your mouse story."

"Gee, Mr. Finley, thanks. I like to write stuff like that."

"For a long time I've been toying with the idea of starting a column for young people . . . school stuff—sports, student reviews of the junior play, funny things that happen in class—things like that. But until I'd read your piece in *The Scoop,* I could never find anyone I thought could write it. How would you like to try? Couldn't pay you anything, but you could have a by-line, and—"

"Pay me? Oh, Mr. Finley, I'd give you a percentage of my allowance if you'd just let me do it."

"We've got a deal then."

He stuck out his hand, and I wanted to kiss it, not shake it. "*The Sentinel* goes to press first thing Wednesday morning. You'd have to have your column in Monday. Mr. Wills said your spelling might need a little editorial attention." Mr. Finley grinned, but I wanted to murder Mr. Wills.

Being a real reporter would change my life. Every kid in Sagamon High School reads *The Sentinel.* My name would be as well known as Barbara Walters's. Liz Ray would probably pop over to my lunch table to tell me what the Hi Gals were doing. It wouldn't be as good as belonging, but a heck of a lot better than being completely out of it. Maybe something hysterical would happen in the locker room, and Beeb would stop me in the hall and say, "How about this for your column. . . ?" They'd ask me to all their parties so their names'd get in the paper.

I've already had a lot of practice thinking about myself as a reporter. When I was a young kid like Lizzie, I used to cut Brenda Starr paper dolls out of the paper. Well, I kept doing it when I was a little older . . . I've still got them actually, but now I won't have to make up stories about Brenda tracking down leads. No more pretending. Sagamon High School was my beat! I was going to *be* Brenda Starr!

I floated back into the classroom past Beeb Barber and didn't even blush. I was Megan ****** Starr ****** Reporter, my braid replaced by a fluff of pumpkin curls, sparkles clinging to the upward sweep of my long eyelashes. I'd wear gossamer and chiffon with sequins—Bible black and sexy.

"Megan's Beat." It looked impressive, even just printed across a page in my spiral notebook. I imagined that when everyone saw how well I could write, they'd want me to run for office and head up committees to decorate the gym for dances and things like that. I like to be in charge of things. I'm pretty well organized, and I can usually get kids to work . . . at least I used to be able to. Sure haven't had much chance lately.

Mr. Wills almost destroyed it all. Just as I was imagining the delicious expressions on Liz Ray's and Beeb's faces when they opened *The Sentinel* next Wednesday night, Mr. Wills said, "Megan, maybe you would like to—"

I believe in ESP now because I sent him the strongest message I could transmit and shook my head, and he didn't give away my surprise.

"—maybe you would like to read the next paragraph from *The Great Gatsby* on page . . . uh, page seventy-nine aloud." He winked at me.

In a clear, confident voice, like a young reporter already showing the promise she was soon to fulfill, I read this passage about a man whose whole life is an anticlimax after his football career at Yale.

Talk about anticlimax! That dreadful bus was the worst. Right back to sober reality.

If I sat in the back seat and leaned back just slightly, no one could see me, so that afternoon I had scrambled out of my last class, even though Liz Ray was in it and I'd always kind of hoped we'd strike up a conversation walking out. I wanted to get on the bus and start on the first item for my column without being disturbed. I should have known better. I'd barely gotten the notebook open when Tom barged in. First he scooted into my seat and pushed me like he was shoving a car that was stuck in the mud. I slammed into the window and made a jagged scrawl across my paper, marking right through "Megan's Beat."

"Thomas Archibald Arnold, you cut it out!" I said it loud. You can imagine how much Tom likes kids to know he was named after his Uncle Archibald.

"Shut up, Pagan Megan. Whatcha writing? Love stories?"

One rainy Saturday when the Arnolds were going to eat supper with us, Tom came over early and we were listening to records in my room. When I went downstairs to fix us a snack, he got into my desk and found the folder where I keep the stories I write. It even says PRIVATE on the front. Lizzie isn't even allowed to look at it, and she can't read much. When I came back with our milk and blackberry pie, he was innocently looking at a photograph album. He waited until everybody had their plates filled and was quietly eating supper. In front of his dad and everybody he started to read this love story I had written in the sixth grade. I had this man kissing the heroine, Evangeline, all over the place, even on her breasts. I was mortified! But Mother stood up for me. Right in front of Ethel she told Tom she thought it was a tacky thing to do to a friend.

I don't know why I can't have a girl for a friend, like any thirteen-going-to-be-fourteen-year-old girl. Betty Sue's my age, but their farm's six miles from us, and Tom's across the field. I've got my cousin Polly, Aunt Marge's daughter, but she lives fifty miles away in Peoria. She's a year older. Polly's okay when she comes to the farm. When she's with her friends, she can be a little conceited.

So I'm stuck with Tom. He can be okay, sometimes. I was going to blow up if I didn't tell someone, so I told him about "Megan's Beat."

"What'll you write about?" he asked, as if he were really interested for a change.

"Oh, exciting things kids do, school events, stuff like that. Got any ideas?"

He squinted one eye and looked around at the bus full of bobbing heads. "Tim Gable grafted this peach and greengage plum tree together. Grew the weirdest-tasting fruit you ever put in your mouth. You could say, 'Gable gives fruit an identity crisis.' " Tom slapped his leg and hooted. He always laughs at his dumb jokes more than anyone else does.

"Get serious, Tom. This is the most important thing that's ever happened to me. Who else besides us even knows Tim or cares about his orchard? Besides, Tim is so shy, he'd clobber me if I put his name in the paper. Next thing I know you'll be suggesting I write about your disgusting calf."

"Hey, that's a remarkable idea. Rudy's going to grow up to be the horniest bull in Sagamon County. Sex sells!"

"Gross!"

"You'll eat your heart out when he's picked grand champion in Chicago next spring, and I sell him for a trillion dollars a pound. What're you going to write about? Beeb Barber chasing a basketball down the boards or how many handknit sweaters Liz Ray's ole man shells out for?"

"Maybe."

"Ha! You don't even know those snobs."

"Maybe that'll change. Everybody'll know the high school reporter for *The Sentinel*."

"We all know you now." Tom gestured around the bus. "Isn't this enough of a gang for anybody?"

"But, Tom, it's like there's a barrier at school that's got a no trespassing sign for kids from the country. We've got to find a way to get around that. It's just not fair."

"Heck, there are more rural kids than town kids. I don't know why you get all out of joint about that Beeb Barber and those guys." Tom threw back his shoulders, pretended he was putting his thumbs behind his suspenders, and said, real cocky, "I'll have you know, today in gym class I did three running flips, and ole Barber couldn't do one."

"That's because you don't have any weight above the neck," I said. Tom's really good at tumbling tricks, but since he was halfway accusing me of being a snob, I wasn't about to pay him a compliment.

Four

* * * * * * * * * * * * *

I ambled down the lane after the bus let me off, sort
of savoring my miracle. Maybe Mother would whip
up a fast applesauce cake to celebrate. I liked it with
lots of raisins and not quite done, just a tiny bit
soggy. Daddy always eats the ends and complains, because Mother pulls it out just before it's ready so I
can have the gooey middle section. Daddy says it will
give me the bends, but it never does.

Maybe we'd call Aunt Marge. Mother called her
when my test scores came back saying I was reading
on a twelfth-grade level, and I was only in the eighth.
She said Marge might as well know her daughter
Polly wasn't the only kid in the family with brains.
Daddy said he didn't know why it took twenty minutes of long-distance talking to let her know that.

I stopped and sat on the creek bridge for a while.
It was time for chores but it didn't seem right that a
famous reporter had to feed filthy ole chickens. Prince
came trotting over and nuzzled my shoulder. Slob-
bered all over my blue shirt, but that was all
right.

I could see our farm spread out before me. My

grandfather built the whole kit and kaboodle when he married my grandmother. Daddy's right; he was an orderly man. When Daddy says that, Mother always adds he'd also been an ole grouch. I guess he must have been both. Our outbuildings are built from the same model and are all wedding-gown white. The barn's bigger than a church and has a hooped roof. All the other buildings are just a scaled-down version of it, even the little milkhouse. When I'm a famous reporter, they'll probably send me back here with a photographer. I'll make them take my picture in a floaty dress and a big picture hat, swinging on Lizzie's swing under the maple tree, and maybe another one with my arms around Prince.

My grandfather had picked out a good setting. Maybe he'd had a premonition that even if Mother weren't a good farmer's wife, she'd provide him with a famous granddaughter.

When Mother and Daddy got married, they had to live with Grandfather because my grandmother was dead and he was awfully old. He was a stern old man. If you can believe it, he used to knock on the wall between his bedroom and my parents' and tell them to stop giggling. I would have died! Mother can still work up a head of steam thinking about it. She always says that if Grandfather hadn't died when he did, I'd never have gotten born. Even Daddy laughs when she says that.

Lizzie must have been watching for me, or else Daddy had seen me woolgathering and sent her to get me. When he found out about my column, he was going to be surprised. Kind of proud, too, I hoped. Lizzie was tearing down the hill fast as she could move, waving like a maniac. I have to admit she's kind of cute, even if she is pretty chubby.

"Megan, Megan!" She tripped on a rut, fell flat, but got up fast and kept coming. "Come and see what Mommy's got. She had it delivered and didn't tell a soul. Daddy's hopping mad!"

Even before we got to the house, I could hear Mother singing "Danny Boy." That would soften Daddy up. I had been dragging Lizzie along with me, but when I heard piano music, I ran.

She had finally done it! Mother had wanted a grand piano with a smooth, shiny top big as the south forty as long as I could remember. Every year something would happen, a drought or a flood would ruin the bottom ground, hogs would go down, or bugs would get the beans. So there was never enough money left for it.

I just stood there feeling like my heart weighed five hundred pounds. Even if they stopped fussing long enough for me to tell them about my column, they really wouldn't listen. Megan's miracle. Huh. Some miracle. They weren't going to pay attention to me. It wouldn't even do any good to tell them.

I went out and sat on the porch and chewed on the end of my braid. I always do that when I'm worried or mad. Lizzie came puffing up the steps and plopped down beside me. Well, at least I could tell her.

"Lizzie, something wonderful happened to me to-day. I'm going to get to write a column for *The Sentinel,* and probably all the kids—"

She covered her ears and stuck her tongue out at me. Her face was red, and her knees were all covered with dirt. She looked as indignant as Queen Victoria.

"You dragged me in the dirt. You ran off and left me," she said, sticking her chin a mile in the air.

Well, I could stick mine in the air too. When I had a by-line in *The Chicago Tribune,* maybe this family would finally start paying attention. I ran up the stairs to my room and slammed the door. When Mother called for me to come down and see the piano, and Daddy said I better feed those chickens and give Prince some hay, I pretended I didn't hear them. Families are the pits.

I put a record on loud and sat down at my desk. I had to start a new page in my notebook, thanks to Tom. I spent a long time printing "Megan's Beat" in the middle of the clean sheet. After I had chewed about an inch off my braid, I panicked. I didn't have a thing to say! Nothing. Zilch. Zero. What was I going to do? I'd have to call Mr. Finley and tell him it was awfully nice of him to give me the opportunity, but my brain had wrinkled up. But I couldn't do that! This was my one chance. Opportunities don't come in herds.

How could I even have thought I could do this? At Heckathorne I knew who everybody liked, who was smart . . . even some things about their families I shouldn't have—like Betty Sue's older brother serving thirty days in the county jail for siphoning gas out of Tim Gable's daddy's tractor all last summer. Heck, at SHS I hardly even knew anyone's name. Mr. Finley had made a bad mistake.

I took the picture of Beeb I'd cut out last year off my bulletin board, thinking maybe he could inspire me. It wasn't as big as my thumb. You couldn't even really tell what he looked like. No matter how hard I stared at it, my mind was as empty as the notebook paper in front of me. Mr. Finley could hardly print my dreams of having Beeb Barber for a boyfriend, but make-believe was all I could think of to write about.

The whole school could be popping pills, shooting arsenic, or singing in the heavenly choir, and how would I know? Tom was right. I didn't know those kids, and I never would. But if he thought I was going to write about that disgusting calf Rudy and Tim's weird fruit tree, he was nuts.

I also knew my heart might be broken and my life ruined, but those animals still had to be fed. Dumb farm. It didn't even allow you the time to suffer properly. I went down the outside stairs. My grandfather had a thing for porches. On the second floor there's a great big one all across the back of the house. Daddy said grandfather used to sit up there and look out over the fields. I never could see what was so fascinating about watching corn blow in the wind, but today I was glad the porch was there. I didn't want to go down and have to get involved with the piano. Seems it never fails. Every time I have something on my mind that needs everybody's attention, something else gets in the way. You'd think my problems didn't count.

But I couldn't put my chores off forever. Chickens first. I hate those beady-eyed squackers. When I was little, a rooster jumped up on my shoulder and flogged me. It scared me to death. I know it's silly, but to tell the truth I've never felt comfortable in the chicken yard since. Daddy says to confront your fears and they'll disappear. Fiddlesticks. I've been walking in here every night and morning practically all my life, and I still always feel as if that ole rooster is behind me. Yuck!

I threw down enough hay from that loft to give Prince a stomachache. I didn't want Daddy to have any doubts I'd done my chores. He couldn't miss that pile. Actually it looked pretty inviting. I lay down in the middle of it. My hair would be a mess, but I didn't care. Six o'clock. Basketball practice was probably breaking up. Beeb and Mike were probably going home at a slow gait, tired after running around the court like maniacs. They'd have showered, and that gold streak in Beeb's red hair would be glistening. They'd be wearing their crimson sweaters, even if it was too hot. If you've earned one, you've got to wear it. It's sort of like a uniform.

The Hi Gals had probably left Kramer's Drugstore about an hour ago, pairing off. Everybody'd have someone to walk home with. Pris White lives on Elm Street, too, so she'd probably walk with Liz Ray. They'd go up to Liz's room and listen to records, do their homework together, talk . . . or maybe they'd sit out on the porch and wait for the guys to come home from practice. I would. Of course, I couldn't write a column about what I'd like to do. Mr. Finley wanted the facts. I wonder how he thought I'd get them.

I sure wasn't going to find leads for stories fooling around in a haystack. I sneaked up the back stairs to my room and wouldn't go down for supper, even though I could smell biscuits baking. I pretended I had a headache. Mother tried to persuade me to eat, but Daddy said I would when I got good and hungry. He'd let his own children starve. I thought Mother might make more of a fuss, but I guess all she could think about was her dumb ole piano. It seemed to me when their kids got into a mess like this, mothers would get a special message, kind of like a telegram from their heart.

Before she got sent to bed, Lizzie brought me a biscuit smeared with some strawberry jam she'd helped to make. I still hadn't thought of one line for my column, and I told her I had too many problems to be worried about food. I ate it when she left, but cold biscuits, even as good as Mother's, won't win any prizes.

I cried myself to sleep, and the next morning I really did have a headache. My eyes were swollen and stuck. I had to bathe them open. They were as red as Aunt Marge's fire opal. I didn't want to go to school because, frankly, I couldn't face telling Mr. Finley I wouldn't have the column ready for him next Monday. I had the feeling he didn't like quitters any better than I do, but there were only six days left and not one word on that piece of paper.

Daddy did my chores. Mother packed him and Lizzie a lunch, and they went off to work in the timber. I bet Lizzie was a big help. I was feeling lower than a turtle's shell, bored, too, when Mother came in with a tray for two. She'd fried sausage and eggs. We butcher with the Arnolds, but Ethel always takes her sausage home to season. She says Mother makes it too spicy, but it's just the way I like it. The cinnamon-raisin buns were still hot from the oven. It was like a party. We ate in the middle of my bed and didn't give a hoot for the crumbs. Mother didn't ask me what was wrong until we got out in the orchard. Hickory nuts had to be picked up, and we agreed that I'd probably feel better if I got some air.

After we'd filled a two-gallon bucket with nuts, Mother sat under the tree and patted a spot for me to take right next to her.

"Why've you got the blues, honey?" she asked, and put her arm around my shoulders. I hid my face in her neck and cried like a two-year-old, but you can do that with mothers.

When I could stop, I said, "I wanted to tell you guys last night that Mr. Finley has made me the correspondent for the high school. I'm going to have a column in *The Sentinel* with my name on it every week. Or I was going to have, but those kids don't tell me anything . . . and I don't have anything to say." I started to cry again.

"I bet you will before the week's over. I've never seen anything get you down for long." She leaned back against the hickory tree and added, "The first one will be the toughest, but with your curiosity you'll find plenty of things."

For the first time in twenty-four hours I thought I might.

"You know, Mother, this just makes me crazy." I was feeling a little more hopeful about the column, but I couldn't get over being sad. I still felt as if I'd swallowed a lead pipe. "The funny thing is I didn't even know there was anything wrong with being a farmer till I started high school."

Mother laughed, but then she hugged me and said, "Those kids are just slow. When they get to know Megan Morgan, the hotshot reporter for *The Sentinel,* they'll be sorry they dallied around so long."

It was nice having Mother all to myself for a change. Daddy would have given me a lecture about how long the Morgans had been feeding the whole town or how George Washington was a farmer or some stupid stuff like that. Mother knew the kids at Sagamon High School didn't give a hoot about such things.

That night after supper Tom showed up. I heard

the jeep barreling down the dirt road through the field. Our folks let Tom and me drive through the field between the two farms. Daddy says the most damage we could do would be to hit a rabbit, and we've got too many of them anyway.

Mother popped a dishpan full of popcorn. She gave Daddy and Lizzie a bowl and sent them off to watch TV. Then she and Tom and I sat down at the big round oak table in our kitchen like we were having a board meeting. I knew Mother must have talked to Tom or Ethel to get him over here. Since he got that dumb video game for his birthday, it takes a crowbar to pry Tom away from the TV set in the evening. He can sit there for hours and shoot at things. It makes an awful racket and drives me nuts. But Mother has a way of getting kids to do what she wants. For starters she doesn't treat Tom and me like babies, the way Ethel does.

"Now it would seem to me that all the kids would like to see their names in *The Sentinel*," she began. "So I would think that to start with all you'll have to do is find out what clubs they belong to and then ask them what they're doing that's interesting. After that you probably won't even have to ask. They'll just let you know." She gave each of us a sheet of tablet paper and a pencil. "Tom, you list all of the things the boys might join. Megan, you do the girls."

Tom wrote *FFA* and then chewed his pencil. Future Farmers of America. Just what I needed. I don't know what's happened to Tom. It's kind of sad. He was okay until . . . I guess it was around the time we turned thirteen. It was like he got stuck, and I went sailing on by, and it just makes me crazy. He's still so physical, stands on his head, does flips all the time. He always wants to race bikes, almost pulls my braid off my head, pounds on me like a little kid. We're teenagers, for heaven's sakes, and he still doesn't even care how he looks. Like those clothes he's wearing. His jeans don't fit anywhere, and he wears old-fashioned tennis shoes. Anyone cool wears running shoes. It took me about one day at high school to figure that out. I knew Mother meant well, but I also knew her plan was a waste of time. How could anyone who's only interested in cows and video games help me? And Mother just doesn't seem to understand that freshmen don't go up and ask juniors and seniors what's happening in their love lives. Worst of all, she doesn't realize town kids don't tell country kids anything. They don't even know we're there. But something about her faith in me helped. Suddenly I decided I'd have to start seeing Sagamon High School differently. I'd just have to be more alert. Right now those kids might think I'm deaf, dumb, and blind, but I was going to have to show them they were wrong.

Five

* * * * * * * * * * * * * *

Wednesday I went back to school with fresh determination. You would have thought I was Sherlock Holmes the way I watched and listened. I tried to deputize Tom, but he was more like my Watson. Going home in the evening, I'd tell him what I'd seen or heard during the day. Most of the time he'd say dumb things like "Who cares?" but at least he listened. If you want to know the truth, I don't think he was as indifferent as he pretended to be.

I always had my notebook close at hand. When I went through the halls, if I saw a group standing around, sometimes I'd pretend to be tying my sneaker or rearranging my books and I'd hang around and listen. The only problem was, I had trouble getting to classes on time. The first day I had gym I had hung around so long everybody was already finished changing when I finally headed down the corridor to the locker room. I knew I was about to get into trouble, so I took a shortcut and threw open the side door to the gym with a flourish. I almost crushed Liz Ray and Mike Brooks, who were making out in the corner. I could have died!

If I had just moved on, it would have been okay. I could have pretended I hadn't seen them or something, but I froze and just stood there gawking. Mike had his back to me, but then Liz opened her eyes and saw me. She just glared for a second, then she flipped that fantastic white-gold hair with a shake of her head and went right back to kissing Mike. She was so cool. About the only thing I could do was go on to gym class feeling like a freak from outer space. I'd never been so embarrassed in my life.

I had biology fourth period. My lab partner is this new girl named Kitty. Her family lived in Chicago, and her dad was a writer, for money, but then he got the idea he had to write a novel. So he moved the family to an old Victorian house he had inherited from an aunt in Sagamon. I thought it was kind of romantic, but Kitty was really depressed. She said he should have thought about how his family felt about being uprooted from all their friends and everything. Kitty dresses funny. All of her T-shirts have little alligators crawling on them, and she wears cords and khaki, like she was in the army or something, instead of jeans. But she's interesting.

We were dissecting frogs in biology. Kitty and I wrecked our poor frog's heart when we made the first incision. Mrs. Horner got really upset. She said preserved specimens were very expensive, and our lab fees only covered one per team, but we would miss the whole point if we couldn't see how the heart functioned. To tell you the truth, I really wasn't very interested, but neither Kitty nor I wanted to hurt her feelings. That frog's heart really seemed to mean a lot to her. Tom's in our class, too, and for once he helped us out. He told Mrs. Horner to cool out and said we could look at his frog. Then we had to listen to a lecture from her on how rude the children of our generation were and how we had all lost our morals along with our manners. I wondered what she would have thought if she had seen Liz kissing Mike right out in the hall.

After Mrs. Horner settled down, we went back to hacking away at our frog. We christened him Groucho. Tom sneaked over to borrow lunch money. I guess he'd be embarrassed to ask me later on, when we got down to the cafeteria. I swear he's the most ir-responsible kid in this school. We get the same allow-ance, with lunch money figured in, but he always ends up owing me half of his before he even gets started.

"Is he your boyfriend?" Kitty asked when he went back to his table.

"Of course not," I answered her—a little too snappy, but it kind of hurt my feelings for her to think I'd have a boyfriend a foot shorter than me who acted like a child.

We had lunch fifth period. Usually Tom and I just found a seat wherever we could. None of the other kids from the bus had lunch fifth period except Tim Gable, and he was so shy, he ate outside somewhere. His mother packed a brown bag for him. In the beginning Tom wanted to eat out there, too, but I wouldn't hear of that. If we acted like untouchables, for sure that's how they'd treat us.

Kitty walked into the lunchroom with Tom and me, so it was just natural for all three of us to sit together. We were laughing about Groucho and having a good time until Beeb and Mike started through the line. For a change I wasn't feeling left out or awkward, but then Liz looked right through me and waved for Mike and Beeb to come to her table. I had to spend the rest of the time watching Beeb sitting next to Pris White. It gave me a stomachache. He didn't seem to talk much, but she was flirting with him like a maniac. Priscilla was a bubbler and a bouncer. Probably just what he liked.

"The kids at Sagamon sure don't know how to dress, do they?" Kitty asked, looking right at Liz's table. I thought she had to be kidding. I couldn't imagine anything as neat as that crimson sweater over Beeb's white turtleneck T-shirt, and everyone knew Liz's mother took her to Chicago four times a year just to buy clothes.

"What's wrong with them?" I asked, and acted just a bit indignant. After all, Kitty hadn't been asked to join the Hi Gals or sit at Liz's table either. I thought she was probably jealous.

"Don't you have a copy of *The Preppy Handbook*? All of my friends in Chicago had one. Of course, we didn't really need it. We all dressed that way *before* it was published."

47

"What about my clothes?" Tom asked and pulled the lapel of his blue corduroy FFA jacket out for Kitty's inspection. The club emblem was embroidered in bright gold over his breast pocket and *Future Farmers of America* was spelled out in great big letters across the back. I thought Kitty would choke on her sloppy joe.

Right when we were talking about clothes, this couple walked into the lunch room with identical T-shirts, except the boy's had *E* on the front and the girl's had *T*. When they stood together, they spelled *E.T.* I had to explain to Tom, of course, that they were advertising the movie about that little wrinkled guy from outer space. The movie hadn't made it to Sagamon yet, but I'd seen it advertised on TV.

Well, that couple made me start looking at everybody's T-shirts, and I got a terrific idea for my column. Some of the ones kids were wearing were pretty unbelievable. There were revolting ones like *Party Till You Puke* or vulgar ones like *Teachers Do It With Class,* but I picked the cleverest ones—those that would pass the censor—and wrote an item under the caption "Have You Noticed?" I told who was wearing what T-shirt and tried to say something witty about each one. One of the juniors had *The Living End* embroidered on the back of his jeans, but I decided to leave that one alone too.

I must have cured my writer's block, because as soon as I wrote that first item I got a couple of other ideas. Kitty told me she spent the summer at a theatrical camp and had the lead in *Can Can*. Since she was as out of it as I was, I thought I might as well help her out. I wrote,

> *Can this Kitty cancan? Ask the kids at West of Broadway Theatrical Camp in Libertyville, Illinois, who last summer cheered Katherine Wells's performance as a French chorus girl.*

I liked to read that one out loud because I love puns, alliteration, and stuff like that.

One of the chem classes brewed up a concoction that made the whole school smell like a garbage dump. I found out a couple of names of the seniors in that class and wrote this item:

> *Rumor has it that Amy Bloom and Ben Greer won the Creative Chemist Awards for the week. Their mixture of Limburger cheese, Ben's sweat socks, and a Big Mac, which we all had the pleasure of inhaling last week, has been purchased by the Green Fly Corporation for a new bug spray.*

I used *rumor* just in case they wouldn't like the publicity. I didn't want to get sued.

Of course, I wasn't writing about the Hi Gals or Beeb, but I decided it was just a matter of time. When they found out who I was and what I was doing, I thought they'd probably be more likely to start talking to me. In the meantime I was relying on my imagination as much as anything else.

Tom gave me some jokes. They weren't very funny, but my deadline was coming up, and I was desperate.

After Mother reminded me ninety times in one evening that I owed him a favor because he helped me hoe the tomatoes when it was ninety-five degrees last summer, I put his name on this one:

Tom Arnold is available again. Has been since his girl called, and he said, "Our going steady has gotten very monotonous. Every time a girl calls me up, it's you."

The student council election campaigns were going on, and every morning we had an assembly to hear another candidate explain his platform and to watch his campaign committee put on a show. I decided to write a political item. I didn't know any of the candidates because they are all seniors, but I compared their speaking styles to famous people I'd heard on TV. This one guy, Randy Green, gave me the idea because he reminded me so much of Teddy Kennedy. I think Daddy knows Randy's father.

The teachers at Sagamon High School usually seem to think their students watch too much TV, but perhaps they will reconsider after listening to the student council president candidates present their campaign pitches in assembly. Since Randy Green hasn't left town, he must have learned his oratory style from the tube. If you close your eyes, you can hear the breakers in Hyannisport and see the brothers passing the torch as Randy says, "My fellow students, I came this morning in my caah. . . ." Teddy would be flattered. Rose would be flattered.

But even those items weren't enough. I couldn't come up with any new material until I went to English class a day or two later and Mr. Wills had us do a warm-up exercise before we wrote a poem. He asked us to write a whole page of "Can you imagine what would happen if. . . ?" That gave me a terrific idea for my column. I filled it up with stuff like:

Can you imagine what would happen if Mr. Wills didn't give any homework?

He gave *tons* every night. New teachers always do.

Can you imagine what would happen if girls got to use the gym for volleyball practice after school?

Boys always have it!

Can you imagine what would happen if Bonnie Bowles and Skip Blunt didn't go steady?

They're seniors and have gone steady since junior high. He's real good-looking, and they go around holding hands in the hall and making eyes at each other.

I read each item over ten times to be sure there weren't any spelling errors, and the more I read them, the better I felt. Considering I knew hardly a soul in the whole school, it hadn't turned out so badly, I decided.

Mr. Finley worked out with the school that I could be excused from study hall on Monday morning to bring my copy in to his office. The presses on which they print *The Sentinel* every week, as well as wedding invitations, flyers, and that stuff, are in the back; his office is behind the counter where they handle subscriptions and collect social items and ads people bring in. I felt pretty important when he asked me to come around into his office so he could look over what I had written. It had a nice inky smell. I was just looking around, enjoying being in a real editor's office, when he began to laugh.

"What's so funny, Mr. Finley?" My heart sank. My column must be awful. There was only that one dumb joke Tom had given me, and I didn't think that would amuse a sophisticated man like John Finley.

He sobered up and said, "Megan, this is just fine. Just what I wanted. You put in lots of people's names, and that sells newspapers."

He reached in his desk drawer and shuffled through a lot of clutter until he found a small notebook with a spiral binding top. "Carry this with you all the time. Should just about fit in the back pocket of your jeans. See, I'm never without mine."

Mr. Finley carried his in the inside pocket of his suit jacket, but it was just like the one he'd given me. I felt as if I had just been initiated into a club, almost as important as the Hi Gals.

"We're going to turn you into a first-class reporter, Megan. You're clever. Hear you come by it naturally. Your mother works on the election board, doesn't she?"

"Yes, sir. The whole Republican Party would prob-ably just about collapse without my folks. They're always running off to do something political, and Daddy *talks* about it all the time."

"What does your dad think about you writing this column, Megan? Is it okay with him?"

"You know, Mr. Finley, I'm not even sure it's sunk in that I'm doing it. He knows, but the day I told him, Mother had a piano delivered. Daddy thought it was too expensive, but I guess Mother must have figured he would be too proud to have them come and get it. He's huffed and puffed for about a week. Hasn't paid much attention to any of us. But Mother's still got her piano."

Mr. Finley must be a very good-natured man. When I left his office, he was still smiling.

Six

* * * * * * * * * * * * * * *

The Sentinel comes out about 3:30 Wednesday after-noons, but Mr. Finley told me they started printing in the morning, so I skipped lunch and went to the newspaper office to pick one up. I had looked at it there, but with Mr. Finley's staff watching I only read it once casually. I was too embarrassed to look at it at school for fear someone would ask me what I was doing. It wouldn't be cool to be caught reading your own column, so I had only managed one more quick look in the girls' bathroom.

It hardly even bothered me when I heard the Hi Gals planning to play tennis in the city park after school. After my last class I ran out to be sure I got the last seat on the bus. If I kept the paper in my lap, none of the kids up front could see what I was looking at. "MEGAN'S BEAT." It looked really professional. Set in type like that in a real newspaper, my words seemed so different and sounded so much better than when they were in my notebook. I just had never been so proud of anything in my life. Next week my life was going to be different. I'd better start learning how to play tennis. And Tom and I were going to have to practice dancing. He'd die, but now that I'd probably be asked to the student council dances, I sure wanted to be prepared. Beeb might not ask me to go with him, but I bet he'd ask me to dance at least once, just to get to know *The Sentinel*'s high school correspondent. We wouldn't have any trouble finding anything to say because we could always talk about the column. Oh, it finally was going to be wonderful!

When Tom sat down next to me, he grabbed the paper out of my hand and said, "Hey, hey Megan, that ain't bad." Strong praise from Mr. Arnold, I assure you. He even sat up straight and stayed on his half of the seat while he read "Megan's Beat" aloud. When he got to the part about him, he started to pound on me, but I think he was pleased.

Even though we're not supposed to hop around, he jumped up and ran over to where Tim Gable was sitting by himself. "Tim, look at what ole Megan the Pagan has been up to. Writin' a scandal sheet."

Tim's shy, but nicer than Tom. Not so rambunctious. He turned around and almost looked right at me. "That's great, Megan. Glad someone's finally blowing the whistle on Wills." Tim's a sophomore, but he had to take freshman English over. Probably because he's too shy to express his opinion about anything. Tom says Mr. Wills is making his life miserable. Poor Tim'll probably flunk English again, but he's not stupid. He'll probably quit school when he's sixteen anyway. His Dad's got about seven hundred acres of cleared land and needs him at home.

Betty Sue and Dick Krug read "Megan's Beat" too, and the guys teased Betty Sue, saying she could use my column to advertise for boyfriends. Betty Sue always pretends she's mad when they tease her, but I think she encourages 'em. Betty Sue's definitely not cool like Liz Ray or Pris White and those kids.

When I got up to the house, I was out of breath. I'd run all the way up the hill because I couldn't wait to show the paper to Mother. But she was on the phone and put her finger to her lips when I came bursting in calling, "Mother, Mother, wait till you see—"

"Now, Ethel, I wouldn't be so upset if I were you. Your sister tends to exaggerate things. You have to remember Millie's never raised a child of her own. . . . Well, what if people do think Tom's had a girl friend? That's not a crime, is it? Thirteen's not that young nowadays, Ethel. I *know* Megan didn't mean to embarrass you or Tom. Tom's her friend . . . . Oh, but you know that's just kid stuff . . . all kids argue. Well, of course I'm defending Megan. She's my daughter, and I know she didn't have any malicious intent in that column. Besides, just the kids will read it. . . . Well, maybe Millie doesn't have as much to do as the rest of us, no husband or children to look after. Let's just not worry about the column. What did you get for eggs this week? A lot of difference from what people pay in the supermarket, isn't it? Well, listen, Ethel, I've got to go. Yes, I'll tell her how upset you were. Bye."

Mother put down the phone and rolled her eyes. "Tom's Aunt Millie told Ethel you've smeared Tom's reputation, saying he's already had a girl friend and him only being thirteen. Isn't that the limit? Millie's fifty-two, and as far as I know she never did have a steady. That's probably why she's so upset. Now, let me see how my daughter's name looks in print."

Mother and I decided only Ethel and Millie could be so sensitive. Tom's being an only child just made them overly protective. The carnival was going to be in town next week, and I bet we'd have to beg Ethel to let Tom go. I wished *this* year I could go with someone whose mother didn't think we were going to be kidnaped by child pornographers. Like Beeb for example.

Daddy had been cutting brush all day, so we knew he'd come home all tired out and cranky. Mother folded *The Sentinel* so "Megan's Beat" was prominent and propped it up in front of his milk glass. She said it would cheer him up after such a hard day.

The phone rang before he even got to the table, so he wasn't properly prepared to hold up his end when Chick Green called. Chick's the Republican State Committeeman and about the most important politician in our town, maybe even in the state. Daddy thinks he's really something. Spends hours lecturing us on what Chick Green has done for our county and all that.

"Well, yes, Chick, Lucy did mention something about her writin' this thing, but I been pretty busy around here and didn't pay much attention. . . . Well, yes, yes, I did know John Finley asked her to do it, but Lucy said it was just some school thing. I didn't think it could be political. . . . Now, Chick, you know John Finley couldn't influence one of my kids. We Morgans always have been straight party-liners. You know that, for God's sakes. . . . No, no, reckon I didn't know your boy was runnin' for an important office up at the school. Hey, he's a chip off the ole block. He sure won't have any trouble . . . She did? Compared him to who? Teddy Kennedy? Now, Chick, I'm sorry about that. I really am. I can't believe Megan knew it was your boy. Yeah, I can imagine John Finley did know, but you just don't know my Megan if you think he could have influenced her. . . . I'm sorry, Chick, I really am. . . . Yeah . . . yeah. . . . Well now, listen here, if there was some kind of plot, I'll find out about it, you can bank on that. Yeah, I'll talk to her, and I'll sure call you back if I find out anything. Well, sure, I bet he *is* upset. Okay, Chick. I'll be talkin' to you later."

If I hadn't been so tall, I'd have tried Lizzie's trick and crawled under the table. I thought Daddy was going to kill me for sure. But Mother saved me. She started to laugh. In fact, she put her head down on the table and laughed till the tears rolled down her face.

Daddy looked bewildered. He was all ready to let me have it and must have expected some support from Mother.

"I'd just like to know, Lucy, what you find so confounded funny about our daughter wrecking Chick Green's boy's chances for his first election. After what that man has done for this county. . . ."

"Teddy Kennedy! Oh, that's beautiful." Mother wiped her eyes. "I get so sick and tired of Chick's bragging and blowing, and of his controlling. And that kid of his is a first-class smart aleck. Megan, honey, if you can turn the tide of the political leadership in this county, I'll give you a medal *and* an applesauce cake."

"But *Teddy Kennedy*? Megan, why him?" Daddy asked, acting as if even the name gave him a bad taste in his mouth.

" 'Cause Randy Green gets up there, rolls his eyes, flirts with all the girls, and talks like a preacher . . . like this, 'My fellooo students,' " I said in my deepest voice and threw my arms out wide. Mother started laughing again.

"Daddy, who would you rather I'd have compared him to? Richard Nixon?"

"Now what do *you* know about Richard Nixon?"

"My history teacher told us about him. I think he was a mean-minded, egotistical maniac who wanted to be a dictator. He even lied to his own daughter."

"Will you listen to her? Lucy, why you want to educate these kids is beyond me. Better put you out to cultivating corn, young lady."

When they sent me upstairs to bed, Mother and Daddy were still talking about it, so I went all the way up and then took my shoes off and crept back down to listen at the foot of the stairs.

"That kid needs to be taken down a peg or two," Dad was saying. "She's too accustomed to being in charge, and you know you spoil her, Lucy."

"I just love her, Joe. You can never love a child too much."

I started to say, "You're right, Mother," but I'd have blown my cover, so I kept quiet and listened.

"I like Megan best when she's bustling about in that funny, self-important way of hers. I don't want her to be intimidated," Mother said.

"That's not likely to happen to your daughter, you feisty woman. Why don't you come over here. . . ."

There they went, getting romantic again. I tiptoed upstairs and got into bed feeling pretty good.

When the bus stopped in front of the school next morning, I popped off with everyone else. Didn't even check to see who was out there. I decided if I could shake up the whole Republican Party with my pen, it was time to stop apologizing for living on a farm.

My new confidence lasted till I got through the front door. Bonnie Bowles, that senior girl I had mentioned in the "What If" section of "Megan's Beat," was standing there waiting for Skip Blunt, that guy she's gone steady with for about a hundred years. She gave me a look that would have wilted lettuce without vinegar and said, "You little twerp!"

I was so startled, I stopped dead and was going to

ask her what her problem was, but she turned around and all I could see was the back of her head. If somebody hadn't giggled, I'd probably still be standing there in shock. I looked behind me and saw Liz Ray standing across the hall, probably waiting for Mike.

"Megan." She motioned for me to come over. My heart was beating a tattoo. If she yelled at me, too, I was going to pitch it all in. Bonnie was still standing there like an ice sculpture, so Liz spoke softly. "Don't pay any attention to her. She's all bent out of shape because even a freshman knows about Skip's indiscretions. How *did* you know, by the way?"

Liz was looking at me as if I were really clever, and I had no idea what she was even talking about.

"Skip's indiscretions? What do you mean?"

Then Liz giggled. "Oh, that's too funny. You see, Bonnie's been going steady with Skip all this time, but everybody knows he always has somebody else on the sly. Says he's going out with the guys and then takes one of his current interests someplace out of town. To motels and stuff. He meets girls after he takes Bonnie home, but tells her he has to get back early because he can't break training."

"Are you kidding?"

"No, everybody knows about it. Bonnie, too, even though she pretends she doesn't. That girl is crazy about him, so she's willing to look the other way. Bonnie must have thought you were being ironical in your column. I know I did."

"Seems like I've really messed up again." I felt awful, even though I was glad Liz had read "Megan's Beat."

"Hey, don't be silly. I thought your column was terrific." Liz colored a little bit and then added, "Also, I wanted to thank you for not saying anything about Mike and me. You know, when you saw us in the hall the other day."

We started walking down the hall together, just as natural as you please. Guess she'd decided not to wait for Mike.

"Oh, Liz, I wouldn't have written about that."

"Mike was supposed to have been practicing his free throws, and I had study hall. You could have gotten us in real trouble. We'll have to be more careful now that there's a real reporter roaming around the halls."

"After the tempest I've stirred up this week without even meaning to, I wonder if Mr. Finley will even let me keep writing the column."

"Who got upset other than Bonnie?"

"For starters, Randy Green's father called mine and was *furious*! Then—"

"Oh, he would. You wouldn't believe how spoiled Randy is. My folks play cards with his, so I know. And you know, I think he does act like Ted Kennedy. I'm going to vote for Rick Chambers."

"I said he reminded me of Tom Brokaw, but I don't even know Rick."

"He's funny and smart. You pegged him as well as

you did Randy. Don't worry. I think it's really neat we've got a high school column in *The Sentinel*."

"I just love to write, but I'm not sure I know enough kids to do the kind of column Mr. Finley wants." Oh, why did I admit that to her? I didn't have to make a public announcement that I'm an outsider. She already knows that.

"You'll get to know everybody. Don't worry about it." She stopped in front of her locker. "Want to go to the carnival next Thursday night? Everybody'll be there. That should be a good place to be an on-the-scene reporter."

I couldn't believe it! Maybe I hadn't heard her right. Liz Ray asking *me* to go to the carnival with her. Somebody just *had* to bring me into town. I'd kill myself if they didn't. I tried to sound cool.

"I'd really like to. I'll have to ask my mother to bring me in. I can drive, but I don't have my license yet. Could I tell you tomorrow?"

"How did you learn to drive?" She looked as if I'd said I'd taken a rocket to the moon.

"One of my friends and I practiced driving a tractor around the barn lot." I didn't tell her Tom almost tore down our milkhouse.

"My father'd kill me if I got behind the wheel of anything before I'm fifteen, but I'm just dying to try." She started to open her locker, but Liz must be an impulsive person, thank goodness, because she turned back to me and said, "Hey, why don't you sleep over at my house Thursday night? You could bring your stuff to school and put it in your locker until the end of the day."

"That would be super." I wanted to jump up and down and do a jig, but I guess that would have been gross. I was just praying she wouldn't suddenly realize she'd broken the SHS code and treated a country kid like a human being and change her mind.

"Okay. I'll meet you here Thursday after school then." She opened her locker and started digging for her books.

My locker was down the next corridor, and so was Tom's. I met him on his way to class. I grabbed him and danced him in a circle. "Megan Morgan, have you gone even loonier than usual?" He tried to break away from me. "What's the matter with you?" I leaned *down* and kissed him on the forehead.

"I'm just happy," I said, and floated on down the hall.

Tom looked around carefully to see that no one had been watching and then went on to class muttering, "Girls are so weird."

I didn't tell Tom that Liz had asked me to the carnival *and* to sleep over, because he wouldn't understand how important it was and besides he might say something dumb in biology and Liz might hear him. I was going to be late for class, but I had to tell someone. Finally I was going to see what that beautiful house looked like from the inside. Once it had said in *The Sentinel* the Rays went to Europe and brought back "treasures." I couldn't wait to see them!

I dug out a dime and raced off to the pay phone. I was so excited I had to dial our number twice before it rang.

"Hey, Mother, guess what? No! Randy Green's henchmen haven't attacked . . . at least not yet. Liz . . . Liz Ray, Judge Ray's daughter, you know, they live in the big brick house on Elm Street. . . . Did he really? I didn't know you got *that* many speeding tickets. He'll probably think I'm the daughter of a criminal. Do you think he'll remember? Well, I guess if Daddy never has gotten any, that does balance things out. But, Mother, what I'm trying to tell you is, Liz asked me to stay all night at her house! Can you believe it? And don't bother working on Ethel because *Liz* and I are going to the carnival. Isn't that terrific? Mother . . . I can do it, can't I? You're the most fantastic mother in the whole world . . . . Really, Mother, I haven't gotten sick on a ride since I was ten, and then Tom rocked the car. Hey, I'm going to be late for biology. Iron my blue shirt? And wash my best jeans. Thanks! See you tonight."

Biology class had already started when I got there, and Mrs. Horner was talking to the class. I tried to slide into my seat without creating a fuss, but she hesitated long enough to look at her watch and say "Been writing out in the hallway, Megan?" before she went on lecturing about the interesting anatomy of the frog. I didn't think teachers would read my piece. I wasn't so sure that I liked the idea.

Kitty kept looking right at Mrs. Horner, but she

hissed "Traitor" at me under her breath. That did it. I wanted to choke the alligator right off her stupid shirt. She just couldn't be upset. I had said the camp kids *liked* the way she did the cancan.

It was a lab day, so when we moved over to the tables, she told me why she was mad at me.

"Here I am, a new kid in this stupid hick school, and you have to make them think I'm a trashy chorus girl. I want you to know, Megan Morgan, that in Chicago I was on the honor roll, and I was going to be invited to join Tri-Hi-Y if we hadn't moved to this wasteland, where people don't have the sensitivity of a fly, even people who are supposed to be your friends."

Oh, no! "Gee, Kitty, I'm sorry. I thought you didn't care what the kids in Sagamon thought about you, since they're not as cool as the kids in Chicago or anything."

"Since I have to live in this godforsaken hole, I thought I might as well try to get in with Trisha Ponds, Rachel Rummel, and those kids. At least they're intelligent," Kitty said in a dismal voice.

"You want to run around with those brains? They remind me of a bunch of ole ladies running a church social. Rachel even wears pantyhose to school."

Kitty's being interested in that group really surprised me. I guess they're nice enough, but they're all teacher's pets and don't do any of the interesting things around school. What was Kitty worried about anyway? For the life of me, I couldn't understand how I could have wrecked her chances with them.

As if she had read my mind, Kitty said, "This morning Rachel and Ellen Powers walked past my locker and Rachel said, 'We thought you might want to join the Latin Club, but I guess that would be a little tame for a cancan dancer.' Before I could say anything, Ellen said sarcastically, 'Very tame.' I was mortified."

If Liz hadn't asked me to go to the carnival, I would probably have committed suicide before the day was over. Everyone was on my case. I had forgotten the item in "Megan's Beat" about how the girls' volleyball team always had to give up the gym after school for the boys' varsity sports. But, unfortunately, the men's phys ed department remembered it all too well.

When I went to the gym, I met the coach and his assistant coming out of their office. I was looking down, and I noticed what big feet they had. I was just wondering if you had to have big feet to be a good athlete, when the coach said, "Why, Charlie, there's Sagamon's first women's libber. Next thing you know, she'll want to play basketball with the varsity." They just walked right on, their keys and whistles jingling a merry tune, laughing to beat the band.

But when Tom sat down at lunch and started telling me he had heard that the chairman of the English department had called Mr. Wills into his office third period and everyone thought she was talking to him about his homework assignments because of what I'd said in "Megan's Beat," I really got worried. My lunch suddenly didn't look very good anyway, so I just left it and headed for the *Sentinel* office. I had to talk to Mr. Finley. Evidently there was something about being a reporter that I just didn't have the hang of yet.

Beeb must have skipped lunch, too, because as I was barreling across the campus he came jogging by. I almost died. He looked like flowing motion, and I probably looked like an ole cow. I knew my face was red as a flag. But he smiled the sweetest smile and said "Hi." Maybe boys are not supposed to be called sweet, but Beeb Barber gave me a *sweet* smile, and spoke to me for the first time. I felt terrific! By the time I got to the *Sentinel* office I'd almost forgotten why I'd gone.

Mr. Finley hadn't gone to lunch yet and he invited me into his office to catch my breath. "Gettin' any comments on your column, Megan?" he asked, real calm-like. I dreaded to tell him. My comments were going to split his calm like an ax through a rail.

"Well, as a matter of fact, Mr. Finley, that's why I've come to see you. *Everything* in that whole piece backfired. Before Wednesday no one in that school even knew who I was, and now I've got more enemies than Hitler. I really love writing that column, but if you think it's going to make everybody in town cancel their subscriptions or anything like that, I'll . . . I'll resign if you want me to. I don't even understand how I created such an uproar, so I'd just probably do it again next week. But, I want to thank you for giving me the chance—"

My voice cracked, and the more I talked, the more lowdown I felt. I hadn't really come down here to quit. I hate quitters, but being a reporter just hadn't turned out the way I had expected. It was bad enough being a nobody, but being despised was worse.

"I wouldn't be too upset if I were you, Megan. First off, the column's new, and everybody's bound to be curious, and a bit apprehensive. Things will calm down some."

"But you see, Mr. Finley, I don't even understand why everyone is out to get me. Maybe I'm dumber than a stick, but I thought everyone would be *pleased* about what I said about them. I'm just shocked by the way people are carrying on."

Mr. Finley took a couple of puffs on his pipe. He was as peaceful as a river without a current. "How's your Latin, Megan?"

"Fair to middlin', I guess." Actually it was more fair than middlin'. I hadn't even known there was such a language until I started high school.

Mr. Finley pointed to a picture on the wall behind his desk. It was just a piece of old freckled paper with some words written real fancy in gold ink *Non semper ea sunt quae videtur.*

"Things are not . . . as they are to be seen . . . what

they seem always? Things are not always what they seem. Is that what it says?"

"That's what it says, and that's not such a bad thing for a newspaper reporter to keep in mind."

Walking back to school, I thought about Mr. Finley's sign. I guess I'd already discovered things *aren't* always what they seem. If I was going to be a really good reporter and stay out of trouble, I'd better learn to tell the difference in a hurry.

Seven

* * * * * * * * * * * * *

The night before I was going to stay at Liz's house, I was a wreck. Here I had wanted to run around with Liz Ray more than I wanted to be a movie star in Hollywood, had wanted to see the inside of her house from the first time we drove past it, but now that it was about to happen, I was scared to death.

I didn't know her folks, and I imagined everything would be real fancy, her father being a judge. I probably wouldn't know what silver to use or anything. When Mother even puts a salad fork on our table, Daddy wants to know why she's cluttering up the table when a man can't use but one fork at a time. I'd probably be so nervous that I'd have to go to the bathroom in the middle of the night and wouldn't be able to find it. And *what* would I say to Liz? I could just hear the silence when we didn't have anything to talk about. The next day she'd tell her friends, like Pris White, what a dummy Megan Morgan was.

Lizzie came up to my room and gave me her opinion about what I should wear. After I had tried on everything in my wardrobe and there was a stack of stuff the height of a hay mound, I decided I didn't

have anything that looked right. Lizzie was absolutely
no help whatsoever. No matter what I put on, she
would say, "Oh, Megan, you look super!" I wish
everybody thought I was as neat as my little sister
does.

But even Lizzie finally got bored with my indeci-
sion, and when my back was turned, she made a flying
leap and landed right in the middle of all my freshly
ironed shirts. Sometimes I wish I had been abandoned
on a desert island and grown up with only seals and
monkeys to contend with.

After school on Thursday I got to Liz's locker before she did, so I walked around the corner and
waited for a while. I didn't want her to think I was
too eager. I still had some pride. Even before Liz
turned the corner, I could tell that Pris White and
Jane Day were with her. They were laughing and
talking. For just a minute I considered getting on the
bus and going home. I never thought I'd wish I were
on that awful bus, but the thought of walking down
the hall and facing those girls was giving me a stomachache.

I told myself about ten times I was Megan ✱✱✱✱✱✱
Starr ✱✱✱✱✱✱ Reporter on an assignment to do the
Hi Gal story before I actually had worked up enough
courage to dash around the corner as if I had just
arrived.

"Hi, Megan. Just a minute. I gotta find my gym
suit." Liz was digging into her locker like a dog after
a bone. She threw out one sneaker, a poster with a

gash through the middle, a crushed felt hat with a dilapidated feather. Books tumbled all over the floor. She had her head stuck into the locker, so I just stood there like a clod.

Jane was the girl who had told Tom and me to be quiet that first day in assembly, but I decided not to hold it against her. She smiled and said, "I think your column's a neat idea, Megan."

I felt a little better, but Pris just bounced around impatiently and ignored me. I thought maybe she had extrasensory perception and sensed how I felt about Beeb.

"Liz, I suppose Mike and Beeb will want us to go to the carnival tonight, don't you think?" Pris asked, fluffing her hair in the mirror on the door of Liz's locker.

"I'm going with Megan. Mike'll come with the guys," Liz answered as she continued to paw through the debris.

Pris snorted just like Prince.

When we finally got outside, Jane walked across the campus with us, and she talked to me while Pris talked to Liz. Jane was okay, but she didn't seem very independent. I had the feeling Pris had been overshadowing her all her life, and she had simply gotten used to it. When we got to the street, Jane left us. Now I was alone with Liz and Pris.

Did you ever notice how three people just can't fit on a sidewalk? My duffel kept banging into them until I had sense enough to throw it over my shoulder. My throat was as dry as the Sahara Desert, but it didn't matter. I couldn't think of anything to say anyway. What ever made me think I wanted to run around with these kids? I promised myself that if this night ever ended, I'd never complain about Tom, the school bus, or anything else ever again.

Pris was talking to Liz about some Hi Gal project, but she made it clear it was a secret, and she wasn't going to let me in on it. She kept calling it "you know what."

Liz finally said, "That can wait till the meeting Wednesday night, Pris." Pris snorted, but Liz didn't pay any attention to her; instead she asked me if I understood the accusative case, which our Latin teacher had tried to explain to us in class.

It seemed about five days had passed before we got to Pris's house. She pounded her heels as she walked up the path still reminding me of a spirited horse. She even threw her head like Prince when he doesn't want me to put on his bridle.

I swallowed hard and asked Liz, "Do Pris and Beeb go steady?"

"Heavens, no, but Pris would be delighted to know you thought so. Beeb's so shy, he's never taken her out unless Mike and I doubled with them, and then Mike really has to pressure him."

"Beeb's shy?" I couldn't believe it.

"Really! Everywhere except on the basketball court. Isn't that funny? Mike and I began to like each other at the end of seventh grade, but I thought he never would ask me out for a real date. He and Beeb have been inseparable since nursery school. They used to wait until Pris and I found a seat at the movies and the lights were out, then they'd come and sit with us. Mike told me later that was all he could talk Beeb into doing."

"Did Beeb start going with Pris when you and Mike got together?"

"No. If Mike and I made arrangements, he'd go along with them, but he never called her on his own. I don't know why Pris tries to make everyone think they're a couple. We all know how Beeb is."

I felt terrific. Sometimes things are better than they seem. I was even beginning to feel relaxed with Liz, but when we turned up the walk to her house, I began to quake again. If a Confederate soldier had been sitting on the porch with a lady in a hooped skirt, I wouldn't have been surprised. Their yard was terraced and each level was planted with beautiful flowers and bushes. I bet Mother would have traded fifty acres of our best wheat for a garden like that.

The last flight of steps led up to a huge porch with four enormous white pillars. The windows went all the way to the floor, and inside I could see a dining room table that would hold all of your relatives at one sitting. On holidays at our house the men and the kids get to eat first, but the women have to wait because there isn't enough room or even enough dishes. My mother thinks it's a royal pain. I bet the Rays've got enough china for the whole county.

The front door was as heavy as the one at the courthouse, and the staircase just knocked me out. It curled around out in space and didn't even have anything to support it. The chandelier hung on a long chain from the second floor, and there were enough candle bulbs to light all of Main Street. Daddy would have good reason to worry about the light bill if he had one of those things blazing away at four o'clock in the afternoon.

A woman in an apron stuck her head out of a door behind the staircase. She didn't say a word. Just put her finger to her lips and disappeared. She needn't have bothered. I still hadn't caught my breath enough to speak.

"Is that your mother?" I whispered when I had got myself in hand.

"No. That's Annie. She cooks and things." Liz whispered too. "Daddy had to meet with the parole board in Springfield last night, and didn't get home until late. He's probably taking a nap. We'll go up to my room."

As we tiptoed up those stairs I pretended I was floating down them in the swishiest long white dress you've ever seen. Beeb was waiting for me at the bottom with a bouquet of violets and lilies of the valley. He was wearing a white jacket, of course, because I was prom queen and he was my escort. I got so carried away with my dream, I tripped on the carpet and almost fell. I don't know why that tickled our funny bones, but Liz and I got the giggles so bad we had to cover our mouths to keep from waking her dad. I thought it was strange to have to tiptoe around in your own house. Maybe she did too.

The Rays had a four-car garage attached to their house that was bigger than most people's living quarters. Liz and her brother had rooms built over the garage. Hers was a dream! The canopy bed ruffle, spread, and curtains were white but the dust ruffle was crimson and the walls had Sagamon pennants and stuff everywhere. Liz flipped on her stereo and I winced.

"Your dad. . . ." I cautioned.

"Oh, after you make it up here, it's okay. They've got Johnny Bob and me soundproofed. My dad's too old to have kids. We get on his nerves."

Liz said this matter-of-factly, but it made me sad just to think about it. Daddy yells at Lizzie and me sometimes, but I *know* he likes having us around.

"My brother'd get on anybody's nerves. Just wanted to warn you. Best way to deal with Johnny Bob is to ignore him."

"What's the matter with'm?"

"Meanness mainly. Won't study. Gets into trouble all the time. Daddy will *die* when he realizes there's no way he'll ever get into law school."

"Doesn't your father know about his grades and stuff?" I was beginning to sound like an investigative reporter. I sure hoped Liz didn't think I would put any of her personal problems in my column for the whole town to drool over.

"Daddy just thinks he's going through a phase. 'Boys will be boys' stuff. Actually, Johnny Bob is reckless, careless, and irresponsible. Always has been. His character won't change, and it stinks!"

My muscles and my brain had just begun to behave and relax a little when we were called to dinner. Liz and I had been having fun listening to records and talking about kids in school. But walking down that staircase, everything began to tighten up again.

Maybe it's because my folks got married kind of young and had me right away that I kept thinking Judge Ray looked more like Liz's grandfather than her father. He had *white* hair, and he wore his tie to eat in. He was sitting at the head of the table, and I had to shake my head to make the picture of him sitting on the bench go away. People didn't have flags and gavels in their dining rooms, for heaven's sakes, and he was wearing a suit, not a robe. No one would have thought Mrs. Ray was a teenager, but she didn't look so old. She just dressed fancy.

I think they were trying to be nice to me, but I found them awfully hard to talk to.

"Megan, it's nice to have you with us. I know your parents," said Judge Ray. "They're fine people. Your father's one of the best farmers in the county."

I had just taken a bit of a slick thing Mrs. Ray told me was an avocado. It was sloshing around in my mouth, while I tried to decide if I could swallow it without chewing. Judge Ray seemed to expect me to say something, so I just let the avocado slither down my throat and prayed I wouldn't choke.

"Thank you. My father thinks you're a good judge too. He was awfully grateful when you didn't send my mother to jail for driving too fast." Oh, why did I say that? What would Mrs. Ray think of mother? "What I mean is, she's a really good driver. You should see how slow she drives the old Allis when she's plowing, but when she has to come to town she's usually in a hurry, you know."

I was just making things worse. Everybody smiled, and Liz looked as if she was about to laugh. Now the whole family probably thought Mother was an outlaw.

"Your mother might drive a little fast, but she's a good Republican. She works hard for the party. You resemble your mother, Megan."

"Thank you, sir. I consider that a compliment." At least I had to let them know I didn't think she was a criminal.

"Lydia, I'm going to be late tonight. I have some work to do in my office before court convenes tomorrow. You may lock up at the usual time. I'll come up through the garage and use the back entrance to my room. . . ."

His room? But I thought all married people slept together. I thought that was why you got married, so you could sleep together and horse around and not have anyone talking about you. But I guess Judge Ray was pretty old to think about horsing around.

"Elizabeth, carnivals are notorious for spoiled food. You and Megan have had a good meal. Don't eat any of that trash. I'd prefer not having to get up in the middle of the night to have your stomach pumped."

Liz made a face, but her mother said, "Your father's right. Last year, as you recall, John Bob was ill for two days after the carnival left."

"Now you girls have a good time, but it's a school night, so you be home by ten thirty," the judge said.

"But Daddy, the carnival—"

"Elizabeth, that will do. You know the rules," he said, as if the subject was closed, and then turned to me. "I imagine you and Liz won't need more than three hours to get a pretty good taste of the bright lights over there. Enjoy yourself, Megan."

When Daddy said no, sometimes I could make him change his mind by sweet-talking him a little, but with a judge you'd just know you didn't stand a chance. "Now where's John Bob?" The judge looked down the length of the table as if he expected to find him a mile down there at the other end.

"He ate in the kitchen with Annie tonight, dear. He has an early appointment over at school, I think."

Mrs. Ray was pretty in a faded way. Liz and John Bob both got their blond, blue-eyed good looks from her. But they were in Technicolor, and she was more like a watercolor. Oh, but she was fashionable! She had on a silk dress, pale blue stockings, and high heels. Her nails and lips were as pink as a baby's. Even though she was thin, she acted like she had on a tight girdle and couldn't bend in the right places. Our gym teacher would have approved of *her* posture. But she was nice and kept telling me what all the food was, trying to make me feel comfortable, I guess. Watercress soup is the pits, let me tell you. I didn't tell *her* that of course, and I sloshed enough of it around to be polite, I think.

"I *bet* John Bob's engagement is at school," Judge Ray said, and rolled his eyes at his wife. He smiled and almost didn't look like a judge. "Whatever his plans are, you tell him to have that machine he calls an automobile in the garage by ten thirty. Have you had a ride in that contraption, Megan? I wouldn't recommend it, unless your life's insured."

John Bob was about as apt to ask me to ride in that car as the Queen of Sheba, but I had seen it. It must have been an old foreign sports car of some kind, and he had painted it bright green and blue. I couldn't understand why he didn't slap some crimson and white on it, but maybe John Bob didn't have much school spirit, since he was always in trouble there. I felt sort of sorry for the judge, John Bob being his only son and everything.

At home when we finish a meal, I'm usually too full, but I feel good. Tonight I felt as if I'd been through an ordeal. I was beginning to think Liz and I would never get out of there, but finally we struck out across the park toward the bright lights of the carnival.

All through dinner Liz hadn't seemed like herself, but she perked up when we got outside. I really liked her. When I had seen her around town and then at school, I'd always imagined she had a perfect life, but her family seemed kind of strict. I would think it would get to be a drag having to act that formal all of the time. But Liz was terrific. You know how sometimes you're disappointed, like when you want something real bad for Christmas, but when you get it, it isn't as great as you thought it would be? Well, Liz was better than I thought she would be.

Eight

* * * * * * * * * * * * * *

"Let's ride the Tilt-A-whirl first, okay? That'll really get us churning, and build up our courage for the loop. The Ferris wheel will be a good place to let our stomachs settle down after that thing."

Liz was going on and on, practically dragging me through the park because it was getting dark and I didn't know where I was going. I was hoping I had enough money for all the stuff she was planning. It would be humiliating to run out of money with Liz Ray.

"I know every inch of this park. Mike and I meet out here when it's warm enough. Before we started going steady, I used to walk around just hoping he'd come along. You know that old song, 'Maybe You'll Be There'? That's one of our songs now. You can say it's our song in 'Megan's Beat,' but I wish you wouldn't say why."

"Oh, I wouldn't, honest. But it might be a good idea to find out what couples' songs are and put them in the column . . . without explanations, of course. What do you think?"

"Wouldn't it be wicked to say Pris and Beeb's song was 'Pretend'? She'd *kill* you!"

Liz wasn't being mean. She had no idea how just hearing their names together made my stomach lurch.

After we got to the carnival gates, the first thing we found was a place to have your picture taken in funny clothes. "Let's wait till the guys come. I want a picture of Mike and me on that donkey, wearing those ten-gallon hats," Liz said, and headed straight for the Tilt-A-whirl.

We dipped and whirled and bumped upside down with our chests pressed tight against the protection of the car rail. My braid kept hitting Liz in the face, and I always seemed to be taking a bite of her silvery hair. We screamed and clutched each other. I was having so much fun, I thought I'd explode.

Weaving like a couple of drunks, we staggered off the Tilt-A-whirl and stopped just long enough to get strawberry cotton candy before we went to stand in line for the loop. It had tracks for a little train to chug up these incredible hills. The cars seemed to teeter up there for a second and then just fall down the other side and hit a steep curve at the bottom.

Liz's not afraid of anything. When I was lifted clear out of my seat on the last drop and my head popped clean off my backbone, I thought my heart would stop. I opened one eye just enough to see her laughing like a maniac. We flashed by all the lights of the midway, and she looked like a beautiful happy clown. I must've looked like the other kind who's about to cry.

At last the loop eased us back to where we started. I was trying to weave loose strands of hair back into my braid, get my shirttail tucked into my jeans, and stop shaking when I saw Mike Brooks and Beeb Barber standing right where we had to get off. I just about croaked. I looked a mess.

Liz, fresh and perky as could be, ran over to them, talking a mile a minute about how much *fun* the loop had been. Until two minutes ago I had been glad just to be alive. Now I wasn't so sure.

"I want a taffy apple," Liz said, grabbing Mike's arm and steering him toward this stand that had apples on a stick covered with raspberry goo. Over her shoulder she said, "Beeb, you know Megan, don't you? She writes 'Megan's Beat.'" She and Mike walked on, arm in arm. Beeb and I just stood there, dumbstruck.

His face was as red as his hair, and he was digging up the grass with his toe, but he was smiling that sweet smile.

"I liked your column."

"Thanks."

"Guess we better catch up with Mike and Liz or we'll lose 'em in this crowd."

Our conversation wasn't going to change the course of Western civilization, but we *were* talking. Here I was, walking down the midway with Beeb Barber.

Who'd have believed it? I wanted to scream and shout and dance and say "Hey, everybody look at me!" but instead I blurted out something dumb, showing him what a coward I am. "That loop thing almost scared me to death."

"I don't blame you. Mike likes those things, but they give me the heebie-jeebies."

We had something in common.

Liz had acted docile enough when Judge Ray was giving her that lecture, but she was eating her taffy apple like it was filled with vitamin C. Mike handed one to Beeb and me. We looked at each other and simultaneously said "Yuck!" That made us laugh like old friends.

We walked on down the midway eating our gooey messes, and even though I knew Beeb was only walking with me because of Mike, I had never been so happy. He was so cute, and taller than me too—a lot. I hadn't expected him to be so gentle. It kinda gave you the impression he'd be kind to kids and animals, and polite to your folks. Like he was being nice to me even though he'd got stuck with me. I couldn't think of one witty or clever thing to say, but he didn't make me feel dumb or anything.

"Okay, Barber, here's a place to be a star." Mike and Liz had stopped up ahead at a place where you threw basketballs through a hoop to win prizes.

Beeb grinned and blushed again, but he walked up real confident-like and took aim. Then the most terrific thing happened. He was standing there with lights reflecting off that gold streak in his red hair, looking like a model for an ad or something, and he turned around and said, "Meg, what would you like to have?"

Well, I want to tell you, my heart was doing flip-flops and I had to swallow a couple of times so I couldn't say "You." He had just given me a nickname like the Hi Gals all had. What did I expect in one night? I kept standing there, stupid as a stick, until Liz saved me. "Let's make 'em win us one of those hats, *Meg*," she said, and winked at me.

The hats were cocky, just the way I felt. They were made from green felt and shaped like proper bowlers, but these ridiculous long skinny feathers were attached at the back and arched toward the front. If Beeb won one for me, I'd have it bronzed.

He not only won it, but put it on me, tucking my braid up under the brim. His fingers touched the back of my neck, and the hair stood straight up like a field of corn. Mike got one for Liz, too, but he had to buy a second chance; Beeb won mine right off.

"Let's go have our pictures taken," Liz suggested, after she had her hat in place and Mike had assured her she had just the right rakish angle.

I was too excited to talk. The thought of having a real picture of Beeb rather than that little pimple of a thing from the newspaper was almost too much to take in. Mike looked at his watch and said, "Beeb and I promised Coach we'd sell T-shirts in the Sagamon High booth from nine to ten. You and Megan finish your reckless riding and then come over to the booth. We'll have our pictures taken on the way out and walk you fair ladies home."

Mike evidently knew the rules at Liz's house, because he added, "We'll get somebody to relieve us a little bit early so we're sure to make your Cinderella hour. Okay?"

Liz and I started off toward the Ferris wheel, and I was in a glowing daze. Everything might have gone okay, but Liz stopped in front of the slush machine and said, "My throat's parched. What color do you want?"

I chose green. Bad mistake. One rotation of that Ferris wheel, and *I* was green. I clutched the bar of our car until my knuckles were white and had a little chat with myself. *You cannot get sick. It would be humiliating to barf from the top of a Ferris wheel under any circumstances. Sitting beside Liz Ray, with Beeb Barber probably standing right underneath, it is absolutely impossible, forbidden, not allowed. . . .*

For a few minutes I was so sick, I forgot it was Liz mopping my head, forgot that I almost got to be walked home by Beeb Barber. Liz kept waving at the stupid Ferris wheel operator to stop the car. But every time we'd go around, he'd shout, "Hi, blondie. You want a longer ride?"

Frankly I don't remember leaving the carnival grounds, but when we got to the park, I threw myself down on the grass and just lay there with my stomach churning for a long time. Liz was great. She said that after all the junky food and those ghastly rides she didn't feel so great either, that it was enough to make anyone sick. She was just being nice. As a matter of fact, she looked perfectly okay, but it helped me get over being so mortified.

After a while I felt much better, just sad about missing my chance with Beeb and looking like an idiot with Liz there to watch. We started walking through the park slowly. It was pretty there at night. We talked about school, what teachers we liked, things that had happened to us when we were kids, stuff like that. I was surprised at how easy it was to talk to Liz, just like Tom, or almost anyway. I had to explain things to her he already knew, but I didn't mind. I liked telling her about my family and Lizzie. Liz said she hadn't known she had a namesake. We really named Lizzie for Mother's aunt, but I didn't tell her. She said she'd trade John Bob for Lizzie sight unseen, but what really got her attention was when I told her about Prince. She acted as if I had some rare species rather than just a good riding horse. I love Prince better than a lot of people I know, but, still, she really did go on.

"I can't believe you actually have a horse of your own! What color is he?"

"Black as a Bible. Except for one white stocking and a star on his forehead. It's kind of weird. Most horses have four stockings, but I like it. That makes Prince unique."

"Did you train him yourself?"

"I did, but Tom's always claiming part of the credit. Mostly he just got in the way."

"Is Tom your brother?"

"No. Tom Arnold. He's in our biology class."

"The short guy with curly hair? The one Mike says is such a good tumbler?"

"That's him. His house is just across the field from ours. We've been friends since we were babies. Shared a playpen, I think. Tom's got a horse named Cricket, but she's old and not very peppy. Tom's more interested in cows for some crazy reason." I wrinkled my nose.

"I've never had a pet. Daddy won't allow animals in the house. Mother has allergies, and he's afraid it'll make them worse."

"Guess they are better off in the barn. I never even thought about having an animal in the house."

"I picked up a stray kitty when I was little. She scratched me to pieces, but I brought her home anyway. She threw up on the carpet and clawed a hole in the drapes before anyone found out I had her. None of us could do a thing to tame her. Daddy finally had her chloroformed to put her out of her misery. I guess she was crazy, but I still cried all night."

If Judge Ray had caught a whiff of my clothes when I came into his house, he'd probably have had *me* disinfected, I thought. I was so embarrassed.

"But I go to camp every summer, and I ride every day," Liz went on. "Sometimes they even let me help out in the stables. I have a whole scrapbook of horse pictures and a collection of wooden and china horses. You don't suppose I could ride Prince someday? I had lessons at camp."

"Sure. If you'd like to come out some Saturday. . . ." Now why did I say that? What would I do with Liz Ray at the farm?

"I'd love to! Maybe we could borrow Tom's horse and ride together. Wouldn't that be great?"

Cripes! Maybe Mother would pack Daddy and Lizzie lunch and send them off to the timber or someplace. Daddy wouldn't even try to impress Liz. I just know he wouldn't. Probably he'd come in the house with his overalls on and demand that mother fry up some of that smelly ham he cured himself. But at least I could talk Mother into putting on the lace tablecloth Aunt Betty made, and maybe if Daddy wasn't around, we could get some of that fancy goat cheese.

"Yeah, that would be fun." I hoped I sounded more enthusiastic than I felt. "You'll like riding Prince. He'll rear up, do tricks and stuff."

We were in front of Liz's beautiful house. Lights sparkled out of the windows, but I wasn't as eager to go in as I had been—I guess because I had been sick and all.

We tiptoed up to Liz's room and put on our pajamas. She wasn't allowed to take a shower at night. Even with the soundproofing Judge Ray might be disturbed at night. I sponged off as best I could, but I really felt yucky. For one silly minute I wished I were home.

Liz piled up a stack of ruffled pillows against the headboard and said we would talk in bed.

When we turned out the lights, I told her everything I could about Prince—how little he was when Daddy brought him home as a surprise, how he had once stepped on Lizzie's foot and refused to move, even though she was screaming like a siren. I thought Liz was asleep, but then she said, "Gee, Megan, you're so lucky."

While I was lying there talking to her just like she was my best friend, it seemed like it was true. I felt luckier than I had since school started.

Nine

* * * * * * * * * * * * * *

The next day at lunch Tom and I hadn't even set our trays down before I was confessing all the gory details of my Ferris wheel experience.

"And you've always told your mom I rocked the car and made you sick on the Loop-O-Plane at the state fair. Phony!"

"You did! But, Tom, you don't know how embarrassed I was, *and* if I hadn't gotten sick, Beeb would have walked me home." I took out my notebook and flipped to my carnival notes. "How do you think this sounds? 'Coach says Mike Brooks is the most conscientious basketball player at Sagamon High. He even saw him practicing his free throws at the carnival the other night. Maybe coach needs to give the team some new incentives. Liz Ray looks pretty sharp in the hat Mike won for her by sinking all those shots.' Of course I can't say anything about Beeb winning one for me, but it's kind of like I'm sending him a coded message, don't you think?"

"Hey, Megan, come and eat with us." Liz was waving from her table.

I started to get right up, but then I sat down again. "There's two places, Tom. Let's move over."

"I don't want to eat with all those girls. They'd give me indigestion."

"Oh. Okay . . . I'll . . ."

"Go on over there. Who wants to eat with someone who can only talk about barfin' when I've gotta eat this stuff?" Tom said, and pointed to the usual boring school lunch.

"Sure you don't mind?"

"Naw, without you around maybe I can get some firsthand pointers on becoming a preppy from ole Cancan Kitty."

"Gross," I said over my shoulder, and moved my tray to Liz's table. I took the seat facing the other way, even though it meant sitting next to Pris White. For some reason I didn't want to have to watch Tom. I knew he didn't care that I'd moved, but I couldn't help but feel a little bit like a deserter. Up until now he had been eating in the lunchroom with me rather than going outside with Tim.

When Kitty came in, she saw me and hesitated. I know she was expecting me to ask her to sit with us, but if I did, then Tom would have to eat by himself. I just waved, and she went over and sat with him. I don't know what was the matter with me. Instead of just being glad to be sitting where I was, I felt about as close to throwing up as I had on that Ferris wheel. Maybe I was developing an ulcer.

Jane watched Kitty walking away and said, "Eat a

preppy and save an alligator." I pulled out my note-book and wrote it down, but I didn't really think it was very funny. Pris kept flouncing around till I was sure she would make me spill my chili. She finally asked Liz, "Where are Mike and Beeb? Of course, we don't have any place for them to sit now."

That Pris's meaner than a snake. Deserting Tom and feeling like a rat just to sit with *her* shows how bright I am.

"Coach wants them to work on a play with the B squad this period. They're not going to eat till seventh today." Liz's eyelashes just flickered, but I knew it was a wink for me. It was the first time I'd felt good since I sat down.

Mickey, another one of Liz's friends and also a Hi Gal, watched me writing and said, "Megan, I just *love* 'Megan's Beat'! You might want to mention some of the Girls Athletic Association activities sometimes. You know since you already gave the coach a dig about not letting the girls have the gym—"

"And since Mickey hopes to be the first freshman girl ever to be elected president of the GAA," Pris said, and raised her eyebrows almost to her hairline.

I thought Mickey looked kind of hurt, but no one else seemed to pay any attention to Pris. Guess they were just used to her.

"Sure I'd like to write something about the GAA, Mickey," I said, "but I don't even know what you do."

"It's fun, Megan. We meet for an hour after school on Wednesday," Liz explained. "The rest of us just horse around, playing volleyball or tumbling, but Mickey's really a good athlete. You should see this girl on the trapeze."

"Why don't you join, Megan?" Mickey asked. "It's open to anyone who's interested."

"Thanks, maybe I will." I didn't even bother to explain that I'd have to try to arrange a way to get home.

Mickey broke the ice, and then everyone seemed to have an idea for "Megan's Beat." I sure wasn't going to have any trouble filling up a column this week. Just during lunch I wrote this much:

If P. T. Barnum could walk into the Sagamon gym on Wednesday afternoons, he would think he had found the answer to his prayers. The lady on the flying trapeze is Mickey Cole, who says if she can't bring up her Latin grades, the University of Illinois will never accept her, so she might have to join the circus.

Anyone who thought we were supposed to give up our bikes with our junior high sweat shirts should see Jane Day put her BMX through its tricks. She has gotten so good at jumps that on a good day she can jump clear across Fifth Street and land on Bill Brannon's front porch without pedaling once. There are some advantages to dating a boy who lives on your block.

At lunch I wrote one about Mickey and made one up. I was going to put Betty Sue's name on it, since I didn't have any items about farm kids, but then I started thinking that Pris would probably get meaner than ever if I didn't say something about her, so I wrote:

Priscilla White had a weird dream the other night. She dreamed that all of the frogs cut up in the freshman biology classes had come alive. She looked out her window, and they were marching down her street. She says she didn't know for sure where those dozens and dozens of frogs were headed, but they'd started toward Mrs. Horner's house.

"Liz, have you been practicing your solo?" Jane asked while I was finishing the frog item.

"When are you going to sing, Liz?" I asked.

"Where have you been?" Pris asked. "The Sagamon Girls' Chorus has given a fall concert ever since my mother was in school. Ole lady Dent would expire if she didn't get up there and wave her arms around like a windmill every year."

"I wish you'd come, Megan," Liz said. "I'll need every friend I've got in that audience to give me courage. Maybe Tom could come with you."

She had included *me* as one of her friends. I didn't care how out of it Pris thought I was. I didn't like her anyway.

"I bet we can. I'd really like to hear you sing." No need to tell her Tom was a Grand Ole Opry fan. He could wear earplugs if he wanted to, but he was going to come with me. Mother and Ethel would probably like to hear the concert too. They wouldn't have to sit with us, of course.

For the rest of the day I only saw Beeb in English. He smiled, but we didn't talk until after class. It about drove me nuts, but luckily we hit the door at the same time. He ducked his head, and his face got red as usual, but he said hello. I started to go on. I still don't know where I got the courage, but I said, "I'm going to hang my hat on my bedroom wall." I had just decided I'd have to take the initiative, since he's so quiet and everything.

"I thought you might wear it to school," he said, and then grinned like we were buddies. "You really look good in it."

Maybe I would. I wondered if everybody would think it was funny or dumb. If it would make Beeb talk to me, I didn't even care.

I couldn't think of anything else to say, and I felt as if my face were on fire, so I just went on down the hall, but later I felt terrific. On the bus that night I told Tom what Beeb had said, but I shouldn't have bothered. All he said was "Too bad he didn't see how you looked when you were on the Ferris wheel."

He wasn't any more enthusiastic about the concert either. I finally had to agree to let him borrow my new Willie Nelson tape for a week to get him to go. He just seemed to be out of sorts about everything. After he'd read what I'd written for "Megan's Beat," he said, "Who cares what those Hi Gal cows are doing anyway?"

As the days passed and his mood didn't get better, I began to think maybe he was mad at me about lunch too. He had started eating outside with Tim most of the time, except when we had pizza. If you want to know the truth, I'd started digesting my food better since he had, but sometimes I sort of missed him. Oh, I mean it was really terrific to have girls to talk to and giggle with, but it got to be kind of boring when they talked about parties they'd had in seventh grade and stuff like that. And, of course, they didn't know anything about what had happened to me before either. Like I wanted to tell them that I'd once struck out Tim Gable, the best batter at Heckathorne School, three times in one noon hour. Tom and Betty Sue still tease Tim about that, but I didn't think the Hi Gals would be very interested.

At least my folks didn't get any more calls about "Megan's Beat." One girl in my English class said something catty about it being a society column, but I didn't pay any attention to her. That night when I was feeding the chickens, I laughed, wondering what she would think if she could see the society columnist scattering cracked corn to a bunch of squacking ole hens.

I didn't mention Kitty doing the cancan anymore either, but I guess it wouldn't have made any difference. Kitty was going to be moving away. She had come into biology class all excited and didn't even try to keep Mrs. Horner from hearing her talk to me.

"Today's my last day here. I wrote to my aunt in Lake Forest and told her my mind would probably turn to mush if I had to finish my education here. I never thought she'd say yes, but we just got a letter. She's going to let me come live with her and go to Country Day, and my parents have agreed. It's a terrific school. Has the highest percentage of acceptances for the Seven Sisters of any school in the Midwest."

I would have asked her who the seven sisters were, but Mrs. Horner gave us a real dirty look. Tom and I talked to her for a few minutes out in the hall after class.

"Gee, Kitty, won't you miss your family and everything, living way up there?" I asked.

"A little, I guess, and I'll miss you guys," she said, but she only looked at Tom, sort of like a lovesick calf, I thought. "But I've got to go. Sagamon just isn't as much like the rest of the world as I expected it to be." She said she'd write to us, and I was hoping she'd explain what she meant by that remark, but Tom was grinning and shuffling around like he'd gone bonkers. I ignored him and promised Kitty I'd write back to her. She'd really been my first new friend at Sagamon. I guess I never understood just how miserable she was.

Later that morning, I had study hall with Liz and Mickey and Pris. We all have Latin together too. Mickey says Sagamon is the last outpost in the Western world where Latin is even still taught. Their folks made them sign up for it, and they both hated it. I got programmed into it for some reason. I didn't tell them, of course, but I actually kind of liked translating those stories, and the grammar made sense to me. Well, anyway, Liz and Mickey usually copied my Latin during study hall. I think Pris probably copied *my* Latin from Mickey's notebook, but there was no way she would ever give me the satisfaction of acknowledging that.

I had just passed my work sheets over to Liz, and she had given one page to Mickey when Mr. Blair, the study hall teacher, walked down the aisle and plucked my papers off their desks like he was picking cherries. He didn't look at either of them, just stared at me and kept coming.

"Megan, I'd like to see you out in the hall, please." Liz, Mickey, and I exchanged quizzical looks, or maybe scared is more like it, and I followed along after him.

He closed the door, and I leaned up against the wall, hoping it would hold me up, because my legs felt weak. He put one hand on the wall just above my head, which bought his face too close to mine for comfort.

"Megan Morgan, you've got twelve cylinders. Do you have any idea why you've opted to put only about four of them to work?"

"I guess I don't know what you mean, Mr. Blair."

He taught junior and senior English. The only time I ever saw him was in study hall. I was surprised he even knew my name.

"I mean you have intellectual potential. I was working on registration when your test scores came in. We were impressed, frankly, because many of our students who come to us from country schools aren't usually as well prepared for high school."

"My mother's pretty smart, I think." I was so confused I didn't know what to say.

"I've met your mother at political meetings, and I'm sure you're right. First of all, I bet she'd be too smart to do someone else's homework for them every day."

I didn't say a word. If he thought I was going to rat on my friends, he was way off base.

"I will be giving these papers to Mr. Miller of course," Mr. Blair said. "No doubt you will all three get Fs, at least for the day."

And Pris would get off scot-free. It didn't seem fair to me. As a matter of fact I couldn't really see the justice in any of this, but who could argue with a teacher like Mr. Blair? He made me feel like a fly caught on sticky paper.

I was late for lunch, and when I arrived at our table, everybody was giggling as if they had been talking about me before I arrived and gotten caught. I slumped down feeling pretty bad about Mr. Blair. Suddenly it was real quiet. Everybody was looking at me and not saying a word. Then I saw the square white envelope propped in front of the sugar shaker right in front of me. Someone had printed MEGAN MORGAN in that fancy lettering, like in the Bible. Inside it said:

is cordially invited by the
sisterhood of
Hi Gals
to become a member of our club
Initiation Ceremony Oct. 3
R . S . V . P .

R.S.V.P.? Were they crazy? Who in their right mind would refuse?

Everybody was hugging me. I was crying. Then Liz started. Everybody was screeching and crying and laughing. It was wonderful. My face was muffled in someone's shoulder, but I heard Tom saying, "What's going on around here? Megan, what's the matter with you?"

I had to bend over to do it, and it embarrassed him to death, but I hugged Tom too. "I'm going to be a Hi Gal!" I screamed at him.

"Oh, for Pete's sakes. I thought you'd hurt yourself. Will you let go of me, or I'm going to punch you? And I think you split my eardrum."

He went back to where Tim was eating pizza, muttering "Dumb girls!"

"Who's that?" Pris asked disdainfully.

"Tom, Megan's best friend," Liz answered.

"Good Lord, does that mean we have to initiate him into Hi Gals too?" Pris shrieked. "My basement isn't big enough."

"He was her best friend *before* she became a Hi Gal," Jane said.

Now I wonder what the heck she means by that, I thought. Being a Hi Gal sure didn't mean I couldn't still have Tom for a friend. Liz understands about Tom. Jane would too when she got to know us better. For just a silly minute I wondered what he was thinking about me these days. I knew that was a stupid thing to worry about, but I just wished he'd stop being such a grouch all the time. I was sure he understood how important it was for me to be accepted by these kids, but he was always putting the Hi Gals down. Sometimes I think he just enjoys driving me nuts.

Ten

★ ★ ★ ★ ★ ★ ★ ★ ★ ★ ★ ★ ★ ★

Mr. Finley handed me the next surprise of the week. On Wednesday morning I met him by the main entrance to the school. He was putting up one of those wire racks where you drop in a quarter and a paper pops out. If it made a weird noise and there was something to shoot at like his video game, Tom would never have made it to classes, but *The Sentinel* was probably too literary to catch his attention.

"Megan, glad I caught you," Mr. Finley said. "Guess you have your readers under control. I haven't seen you lately."

"Hi, Mr. Finley. Maybe my skin's just getting tougher." I reached into my back pocket and pulled out the notebook he had given me. "Your idea about carrying the notebook was great. I've almost filled it up."

"You've done a good job. That's why I'm over here this morning, matter of fact. So many kids trooping into the office to pick up papers, we've decided to put the rack here on Wednesday afternoons. Since you've helped to increase sales, guess I better put you on the payroll. How does five dollars a week sound?"

"Terrific! Couldn't come at a better time either. I'm being initiated into the Hi Gals. Making some extra money will really help. I have to pay an initiation fee and buy a jacket, and my dad's such an ole tyrant about me making sure I live off my allowance. No advances! Course Tom Arnold owes me seven dollars if I can just collect."

"Sounds as if you're in a jam. Maybe I better pay you in cash this week." He reached in his wallet and pulled out a five-dollar bill, my first week's wages.

I had a frantic week. Just in the nick of time I found out we had to wear dresses to the initiation. Can you imagine how stupid I'd have felt if I turned up in my jeans? It gives me nightmares just to think about it. Betty Sue had asked me to get off the bus at her house and stay for supper, but I had to cancel out. She was kind of snippy about it, even though I tried to tell her I just had to have a dress before the Hi Gal initiation. Instead Mother came into town to meet me and we went shopping after school. Daddy had given her money for a new suit, but she said she liked her red one better than the new ones they were showing in the stores. So she used the money to buy me a luscious crimson wool dress with a high neck and lots of lace at the throat. If I ever get to go out with Beeb, it'll match his sweater perfectly.

The next afternoon Daddy had to come to town to pick up winter wheat seed, so I got to hang out with Liz after school. We went together to pick out my Hi Gal jacket. In the army-navy store we found one that was just perfect. It was real big and bulky, but by moving the buttons it fit tight around my hips. Mr. Binnion wasn't very busy, so he stenciled my name on the back right away. Liz said she didn't think it would hurt if I wore the jacket before the initiation, so I put it on and went over to meet Daddy at the feed store.

Sometimes I think fathers should take a course in having daughters. They don't understand anything. I walked into that store so proud, and Daddy said, "What in tarnation do you have on your back now, Megan?"

"Daddy, it's my new Hi Gal jacket." I spun around like a ballerina, so he could get the full effect. "Don't you love it?"

"Looks to me like somebody else already got mosta the wear out of it. And what on earth does it say across the back?"

"Meg. That's my nickname. You'll have to call me that from now on."

"The devil I will. We named you Megan after my mother, God rest her soul, and I guess that's what we'll be callin' you."

Daddy took off his cap and scratched his head. "Don't know what's getting into you lately. Best you just get comfortable with who you are. Trying to change your stripes isn't becomin' to you."

"But, Daddy, jackets like this with a name on the back are what all the most popular kids up at the high school are wearing."

"Megan, it's not surprisin' you'd want to be chummin' with the cream of the crop. I swear, I don't know where you and your mother get your energy."

Daddy looked as if he thought he had a heavy burden to bear. Fathers are so gross. Mother would appreciate the jacket. And I'd like to know what's so wrong with trying to improve on who you are, for heaven's sakes. Daddy and I both pouted most of the way home.

Mickey had asked me to eat dinner at her house and then sleep over after the initiation. Mickey's dad is the junior high coach, so he knows how to talk to kids better than Judge Ray, but he sure does have some strange ideas about what you're supposed to eat. He thinks pork and beef will kill you, so we had this grayish hamburger thing made out of soybeans and rice. I piled catsup on top of mine and got it down. If his theory was right, all of us Morgans would have died in our beds years ago. We have meat three times a day at home, but I didn't tell him that. No use coming to someone's house and acting like a crusader.

At Mickey's you could take a shower anytime you could get in the bathroom, but she had three little brothers and one bathroom, so getting in there was the trick. They could have used some soundproofing too. It was like a zoo. When it got real bad, Mickey's dad would blow this whistle he wore around his neck.

Just when I was combing my hair, the littlest brother came marching right in and used the john. I didn't know what to do, but he didn't pay a bit of attention to me, so I just pretended I didn't see him.

The ceremony was held in Pris's basement, which had knotty-pine paneling and a bar with tons of liquor. Her dad is really kind of awful. He flirted with all of us like he was a kid, but I bet he's at least thirty-five. Liz says he's a district sales manager. I sure wouldn't buy anything from him.

But the ceremony was absolutely beautiful. They turned off all the lights and just had candles on the table where the officers sat. Liz is president, so she read the oath, and then I had to put my hand on the Bible and promise to live up to it. It said we were supposed to love and support all the sisters. I crossed my fingers and said to myself, *All but Pris.* Then I said I would.

There's a secret Hi Gal handshake, just like in college sororities, so I went down the line and everybody shook my hand and gave me a tea rose. When I got to the end, I felt like an actress on opening night. I had a bushel of flowers. Then we sang this Hi Gal song Jane had written. It was so impressive, it made tears come to my eyes. After that someone turned on the lights, and they all began screaming and jumping around, hugging me and calling me sister. It was wonderful.

The whole thing didn't take very long, and even after Pris's mom served us pizza and Cokes, it was only eight thirty. We sat around for a while, and they told me some of the things they had done at other meetings.

Being initiated into Hi Gals was just about the most exciting thing that has ever happened to me, but I must admit I had some second thoughts later on. It all began when Pris said, "Did you guys all know about the governor's conference they're going to hold in Springfield? It's to develop leadership, and all the high schools in the state are supposed to elect a delegate." The girls were listening to her every word, just like they always do. "Of course, the school's supposed to pick someone who shows leadership potential already. I think the Hi Gals should back someone from the group, don't you?"

"Got anyone in mind, Pris?" Liz said, and I thought maybe she grinned at me.

"Well, we're *all* leaders, most of us anyway," said Pris. Now why did I think she meant I wasn't? I couldn't let her make me paranoid. "But Mickey's all wrapped up with GAA. Liz, you've got the concert coming up. . . . I guess I better do it. You know, just so we have a candidate for sure."

Everybody looked at me, but it was Jane who said, "Now that Megan's a Hi Gal, she can use her column to help with your campaign."

Give me a break, Jane, I thought, but, of course, I couldn't say I wasn't going to back one of my sisters, not on the very night I was initiated into the club. What a pickle to be in. Pris'd be about the last person in school I'd want as my leader. I was trying to tell myself Mother was a good Republican even though she didn't think Chick Green was so great, but I still didn't feel any better about Pris.

I was really worrying about that conference until Jane came up with something that was even more horrendous. I couldn't believe it when she said, "Hey, you guys, why don't we pierce our ears? You can do it with a needle and a cork. We'll put thread in the holes and when they heal, we can all get those little gold hoops. They could be like a Hi Gal symbol, since we don't have pins or anything like they do in sororities."

"What a great idea!" Pris said. "I know how to do it. Mom pierced Sally Carter's, and I watched her." She ran upstairs to get the equipment, and I was considering hiding under the couch.

Now I had taken my oath seriously and everything, but I have to tell you, about the last thing in the world I wanted was a big ole hole in my ear, especially with Pris on the other end of a red-hot needle.

As it turned out, I had cause to be grateful to Jane. She saved us by volunteering to go first. After all, it had been her idea, and besides she'd been Pris's devoted slave since nursery school. Pris sure was eager to stab somebody with that needle. She put a cork behind Jane's ear and poked that thing right through her earlobe. I closed my eyes so I wouldn't have to watch. If I barfed again, Liz would think I had a fatal disease.

Believe me, I opened them quick when everyone started screaming and Pris's mother came running down the stairs. Jane was out like a light. Fainted dead away. It was awful! Blood was running out of her ear, and she was white as death. I was so scared. Somebody called her mother, and the meeting ended in a flurry.

Mickey and I had a terrible time getting ready for school the next morning. They really needed another bathroom in that house. I was running late, but when I finally got there and was shoving all of my junk into my locker I saw Betty Sue and her cousin Effie walking up the hall with this guy who really has a bad reputation. He rides a giant black motorcycle, and he dresses as if he's trying to look like one of those tough guys in the California cycle gangs they're always showing on TV. Some of the kids said he even took drugs. Even though everyone at Sagamon thought he was a creep, there was Betty Sue giggling at him as if he were a first-class prize. Betty Sue could be dizzy, but her folks are real nice, and they'd just die if they saw her hanging around with this guy.

When they got close to my locker, I heard him say, "Okay, I'll meet you behind the machine shed down the road from your house about nine o'clock. Now don't you chicken out." He turned off and went down the hall, but Betty Sue and her cousin came toward me. Effie noticed me and said, "Betty Sue, if you don't want your mom to know about him, you shouldn't have let Megan see you. She'll spread it all over her column."

"Don't worry about it." Betty Sue shrugged her shoulders and looked right at me. "Megan only writes about the fancy crowd now."

"I won't tell on you, Betty Sue, but that guy's big trouble."

"You know your mother would skin you if she ever finds out," Effie said and looked at me suspiciously.

"No chance of Megan telling my mom either. She doesn't have time to come to our house anymore." Betty Sue tossed her head in a real snotty way and went on down the hall.

I wondered why she'd got up on her high horse like that, and I decided I'd better talk to her on the bus going home to see if I couldn't find out what was bugging her. I glanced at my watch and realized that I was late, so I took off for my first class.

I had such a busy day, I didn't think any more about what Betty Sue had said until after school. When I got on the bus, I was wearing my Hi Gal jacket, of course, but I had all this other junk to lug home. Books, my dress in a garment bag, my duffel. I was late, so Tom was sitting with Tim, but I needed a whole seat for all of my stuff anyway. Betty Sue was sitting with Ruthie Doolan and didn't even look up. When I had got everything arranged, I turned around to talk to Tom and Tim, but it felt like December. Tim never says anything anyway, but Tom was just plain ignoring me. Tom can really be a drag. I turned back around, pretending to rearrange my gear. As a matter of fact, no one had been very friendly when I got on the bus, and yesterday when I'd yelled to Tim to wait up so I could walk to history class with him, I'd just thought he hadn't heard me. What was going on?

As we bounced along I tried to think what I had done to turn everybody off, but I couldn't think of anything. For the last two weeks I hadn't said one thing in "Megan's Beat" that could have hurt anyone's feelings. I'd been spending a lot of time in town, but they surely couldn't resent that. Somebody had to break through the barrier, for heaven's sakes, and it might as well be me.

I looked around the bus and thought, *These kids are my friends, but sometimes they sure don't have much imagination.* Like we would have given that same dull ole program for Heckathorne's parents' night year after year if I hadn't written a new skit each October. Everybody had complained, and after I had the idea, everybody had pitched in, but not one of them had ever come up with a suggestion on their own. Well, I sure wish they wouldn't get all bent out of shape, but if they thought I was going to miss my whole high school experience just to keep them happy, they were way off the track.

Dick Krug and Mattie Elston were sitting a couple of rows in front of me, but I heard them talking about the governor's conference. Dick was saying,

"That dogface Priscilla White's going to run. She'd scare the governor to death, she's so ugly."

Now, I'm not fond of Pris, but she's sure not homely.

"Megan'll help get her elected. She'll write about her in her column, you can bank on that," Mattie said.

I wanted to put my hands over my ears. Here I was wearing a jacket that said *Hi Gal* across the back. How could I admit to Dick and Mattie I didn't want Pris to represent Sagamon at that conference either? I just didn't know what I was going to do.

Seemed as if it took us forever to get home, but when I could see our house down the road, I suddenly had an idea. I turned around and said, "Tom, I've got all this stuff to cart up the hill. Will you get off at my house and help me carry it?"

"I gotta get home to feed Rudy."

"Big deal. That takes about five minutes. I'll take you right home in the truck."

"Haven't got time." Sometimes Tom can set his jaw and look just like Ethel when she doesn't approve of something.

"Come on, Tom, help a lady in distress," Tim said. "Maybe she'll say in 'Megan's Beat' that you're a white knight." Tim always did have a better disposition than Tom.

"Megan doesn't clutter up that fancy column with any of us. She's got classy town friends now," Tom said, but he got up and picked up my duffel bag.

So that was it. I hadn't put any of the bus kids in my column for the last couple of weeks. There had just been so much other stuff going on. They were mad. Sometimes I wonder why I'd ever said I'd write that stupid column. All it seemed to do was get me into trouble. I took one last look around the bus. I'd grown up with these kids and thought they'd understand. I felt lousy.

Tom was stalking along as if that duffel weighed an even ton and he were making the supreme sacrifice. Mother is smart. She says men are bigger babies than either of her kids. But she can always handle Daddy, and I know how to get around Tom Arnold.

"Want to go fishin' Saturday?" I asked him.

He gave me a quick look to see if I was serious. He's spent three-quarters of his life begging me to go sit by some mudhole. But he wasn't about to come off his high horse too easily.

"Might. Don't have any bait though."

"I'll dig the worms. Daddy says the catfish are biting in the creek."

Frankly, I think any kind of fishing is about the boringest occupation man ever applied himself to. What was so great about sitting like a lump for hours? But seeing as how I'd hurt Tom's feelings unintentionally, I guess I could sit there for a couple of hours and hope I wouldn't catch one of those slick old catfish that I hate to have to take off the hook.

Saturday dawned bright and clear, not a rain cloud in sight. After I did my chores, I took the spade out in the orchard and dug a can of worms. Mother insisted on frying a chicken, even though I tried to tell her I'd be home by noon. She said I hadn't seen much of Tom lately, so maybe we'd want to stay longer than I thought.

At least when we started off, he was in a better humor. He kept running ahead of me doing flips and landing on his feet. You would have thought he was practicing to be a circus clown. We always look up and down the creek and then end up in the same spot. A big boulder sits on the creek bank, but erosion has eaten away some of the earth, so part of it hangs out over the water. Tom was leaning up against one side, and I was lying on my stomach on top of it. The sun had warmed the rock, and it was really comfortable.

Finally I propped myself up on my elbow and looked down at Tom. "You mad at me?"

"Yep."

"Haven't got any good reason."

"You're gettin' to be a snob, just like those snotty Hi Gal friends of yours. Really think you're hot stuff. All the kids on the bus say so."

"That's a lie, Tom Arnold! You're just jealous because you're not doing anything at school."

"Doin' everything I want to. You know, Megan, you always did have more energy than a herd of elephants."

"We bus kids have to become more visible at school. That's the only way we'll ever get any power.

Wouldn't you like to play sports or be in the marching band or something?"

"They don't have a gymnastics team," he said, talking to me as if I were a halfwit. "I'm not big enough for sports, and I don't give a hoot about any instrument except the guitar, and they don't march very well."

I sat straight up on that rock. I had a *terrific* idea! "I've got it! You and I will go out for cheerleading. Oh, Tom, wouldn't that be fantastic?"

"Megan! Boys don't go out for cheerleading."

"Don't be dense, of course they do. I've seen 'em on TV. And you'd be super. You can already do flips and cartwheels." I peered at him over the edge of the rock, but he wouldn't even look at me. "Do you think you could teach me?"

"I'm not gonna try because I'm not going out for cheerleading, for Pete's sake. Can't you get it through your head that I don't want to run around with those snotty kids like you do? I'd rather hang around with people I know, or who like to do things I do."

"Like what?"

"Cattle. Engines. Me and Tim're going to build a motorcycle out of spare parts."

"Outta sight!"

"Don't be sarcastic."

"Come on, Tom, you're much too sensitive these days. Listen, you've got to stop being such a pill and help me."

"Like what?"

118

"The concert Monday night, for starters. You already promised you'd go. Remember I told you Liz was singing in it? Anyway, everybody's going and they'll all have dates. I can't sit there by myself, and I have to write it up."

"What'll you do for me?"

"You should be a horse trader! I'll . . . help you make Rudy a grand champion." Messing around with Rudy was worse than catfishing, but I was desperate.

"Will you wipe out what I owe you for lunch money?" Tom asked.

"Knock it off! That's too much, and, besides, I need that money."

"Hey, you got a bite!" Tom yelled.

Oh, no! That ended our conversation, but at least he hadn't said he *wouldn't* go to the concert.

When we picked him up Monday night, Tom actually looked pretty respectable. I'd kept my bargain and spent half the weekend brushing that lump of a bull calf. I guess he was planning to play fair. He was wearing a sports jacket and had even made an attempt to flatten his hair down. It was all wet.

Mother did her part and waited until we were inside the concert hall before she got out of the car. No other freshman has to go everyplace with her parents. Liz was watching and motioned for us to come sit with them. Just as I'd feared, Liz, Mike, Beeb, and Pris were all sitting in a row. I sat next to Pris, and even in my new crimson wool dress I felt like a sad sack. Tom sat on the other side of me and looked as miserable as I felt. Mickey and her boyfriend came next. Mickey started talking to Tom, and after a while he seemed to be having fun.

The junior and senior girls sang first. Pris kept grabbing hold of Beeb's arm and whispering something in his ear. I would have enjoyed strangling her. Then Mrs. Dent sounded a chord, the lights dimmed again, and Pris, Liz, and the other freshman and sophomore girls in the chorus went up on stage. That left me sitting next to Beeb. For the first time I didn't mind not being able to carry a tune very well.

During the second number the house lights were turned out completely, and each singer held a candle. I'm sure it must have been impressive, but I didn't pay one bit of attention. All of a sudden I felt Beeb sitting *right* next to me. He had scooted over across the empty seat. Without really meaning to, I moved my right hand out of my lap to my side. When Beeb took hold of it and sort of hid our joined hands under the full skirt of my crimson dress, I want you to know I felt as if all the zippers that hold me together had come loose. It was the most thrilling feeling I've ever had. My heart was in my mouth. What if he let go? What were we going to do when Pris came back? Could anybody see us?

The rest of the chorus took two steps back, and Liz stepped into the spotlight. She looked fabulous. Her periwinkle-blue silk dress was just the color of her eyes, and the spot made her hair shine even more than usual. Cornflowers are my favorite, and that's just what she looked like. When she began to sing "To-morrow," Tom punched me in the ribs with his elbow and said, "You better write that down in your notebook."

"I'll remember," I whispered. Beeb squeezed my fingers and moved back over next to Mike just before the lights went up. Wow! Would I ever remember!

Eleven

* * * * * * * * * * * * * *

I don't know exactly what I expected the next day at school. I mean, I knew Beeb wasn't going to meet the bus and get down on his knees and ask me to go steady or anything, but I expected things to be different . . . better.

When I went to English class, my hands were perspiring and I felt real funny inside. All that happened was that I smudged my theme. Beeb and Mike were already in their seats, talking up a storm about something. They didn't even notice me come in.

Six-week grades came out during homeroom. I got all As except in Latin and history. That helped a little bit, but I was still awful disappointed about Beeb. Tom got mostly Cs, except for a D in English and a B in agriculture, which he calls ag, pronouncing it like he's choking on a fish bone. He was expecting to flunk English, so he was happy as a skunk. Tim got an F again. I'd like to clobber Mr. Wills.

Study hall was after English. Since Mr. Blair caught us Liz and Mickey hadn't copied my Latin anymore. Mickey had suggested we get together before school, but Liz said we shouldn't, 'cause now that the Latin teacher knew, he'd be watching, and if we all three (really four) made the identical mistake, it would be a tip-off, and it wasn't fair for my grade to suffer. Liz's a good sport. Mickey and Liz both got Ds. Pris wouldn't tell what she got.

There was an empty seat in front of me, and when Mr. Blair finished taking attendance, he came right back there and perched. "How were your grades, Megan?"

"I got a *B* in Latin," I said, and grinned, but he didn't see any humor in that. I handed him my report card, thinking maybe he'd get off my case when he saw all those As. Wrong!

"You got a B in history? Why?"

"Well, gee, Mr. Blair, I don't really like history, 'cause I already know how it's going to turn out."

He put his hand to his head as if I really gave him a pain. If he wanted to know the truth, it was mutual.

"You like to read fiction, I assume?"

"Sure. See, I got an A in English . . . *sophomore* English, from Mr. Wills." *Under conditions worse than you can ever imagine, Mr. Blair. It's not easy to think with a broken heart.*

"But, Megan, can't you see history has an element of fiction because all of us interpret facts differently, even historians. Imagine the difference between a Southern and Northern account of the Civil War."

That was an interesting idea. I'd never even thought about history having an author. Maybe I'd try harder to like it this term.

I spent the rest of study hall working on my column. The writing was getting easier, but the politics were getting messier and messier. You can imagine that this time I tried to balance references to town kids and country kids, but I felt like a juggler more than a reporter. I decided to start out with something super just to get warmed up. I wrote:

> Lots of kids are rediscovering golden oldie song lyrics that still make a lot of sense. Coach says he even heard one of the varsity whistling "I Want To Hold Your Hand" in the shower the other day.

If Beeb didn't get that message, he was dense as a door. Then I started my juggling act.

> If Dick Krug seems disgruntled, what he was overheard saying in history class the other day probably explains it. "When I refused to take my girl to a party wearing only her bikini, she went with a little moron."

I know puns are gross, but I think Dick will like that, and I've got to show those kids I'm sorry I left them out.

> If Mike Brooks thinks all the girls in Sagamon have suddenly become very religious, he should check out his bumper. He had a sticker that used to say "Honk If You Love Jesus," but some ingenious person crossed out "Jesus" and wrote in Mike's name. Effie Carruthers says a tomboy is a girl who behaves as bad as a boy.

was going to use Betty Sue's name, but I was afraid he'd think I was ratting on her about that awful boy who rides the motorcycle by implying she wasn't behaving.

Bill Brannon says the difference between a boy and a girl getting ready for a party is about three hours. Sometimes he just goes home and watches a couple of football games on TV while Jane puts on the finishing touches.

Some parents suggest their kids bring an apple to the teacher, but Tom Arnold's mother sends two aspirins.

'd probably pay for that, but I couldn't let Ethel spook me on every item I wrote, and even though Tom wouldn't admit it, he'd like the item.

I finished up with some straight pieces about grades coming out and an announcement of the talent show the student council was planning. I just hoped no one would be angry. I avoided the Governor's Leadership Conference. Even though everyone was talking about it because it was something new, it still hadn't been officially announced. I didn't even want to think about how I was going to handle that one, but of course Pris went on and on about it every time she got us together.

At lunch Liz asked me when she was going to get to ride Prince. It made me feel guilty. Everybody was making me feel guilty these days. I knew I should have asked her to come out on the farm, but I was still worried about it.

"Want to come on Saturday? You can sleep over . . . if you don't have a date." That was dumb. *She* always had a date. I was the one who was going to be thirty years old and never been kissed.

"Mike'll survive one night without me. I can't wait to see your horse. Do you think Tom'll loan us Cricket?"

"Probably . . . for a price."

Since I didn't have anything else to plan for, I spent a lot of time thinking about her visit. Even Mother didn't understand how important it was though. Oh, she helped me make plans, but she wouldn't think up an excuse to send Lizzie and Daddy away for lunch. As she pointed out, they'd have to come home for supper anyway. She wouldn't agree to wear her red suit either. Said she was glad I thought it looked nice on her, but she didn't think it was appropriate for frying a chicken. I guess an apron *would* kind of spoil the effect. But she promised me that even if she had to drive the tractor, she wouldn't wear those dreadful coveralls. And she said she'd make Daddy put on his new khakis.

Liz asked Tom if we could borrow Cricket. I wish you could have been there. Butter wouldn't have melted in his mouth. He said yes right off and didn't even try to strike a bargain. He's such a phony. Of course I was glad he was being nice to Liz after all the bad things he'd said about the Hi Gals, but if I was the one who had asked, I'd be brushing Rudy till I was fifty.

126

On Saturday afternoon Liz's mother brought her out to the farm in a pale blue Lincoln that looked as if it was brand new. I was so afraid she'd get it all dirty coming down the lane. Liz jumped out with her duffel and didn't want her mother to come in, but Mrs. Ray accepted Mother's offer of a cup of coffee and a cinnamon roll. I was really surprised. They didn't seem to have any trouble talking to each other at all. My mother was prettier than Mrs. Ray, even if she wasn't wearing a blue silk dress and stockings. She had on jeans, a white shirt, a red sweatshirt, and sneakers. Even though she's pretty old, she still looks good in jeans, I've got to admit.

The first disaster happened in the barn. Liz almost went crazy when she saw Prince, but when I threw the saddle over his back she said, "What's that?"

Now it seemed to me even a town girl, especially one who claims to have done all this riding at a fancy camp, would recognize a saddle, for heaven's sakes.

"No, I mean this thing," she said and took hold of the horn.

"You rode English tack at camp, I bet."

She had. Cripes. It's a wonder she hadn't shown up in jodhpurs and a derby hat. Now what was I going to do? I sure couldn't entertain her in the chicken yard until Sunday.

"Well, show me how to do it," she said.

"For starters, don't post. On a western saddle the stirrups ride lower. When you trot, you go with the horse like you were taught, but you don't use all that energy bobbing up and down. And don't hold on to the horn. If you do, the horse'll know you don't know what you're doing and take advantage of you. Ready to try?''

Like I said, Liz's really a good sport. The first few turns around the barn lot I thought she'd jiggle her teeth out when Prince broke into a trot, but she kept trying till she got the hang of it. We rode double to Tom's house to pick up Cricket. Would you believe he even saddled her? The great pretender!

After we spent about a hundred hours listening to Tom explain every spot on that dumb Rudy that was going to make him a grand champion, we headed out. There were a million places I wanted to show Liz.

"Don't forget to take her to Sycamore Castle!" Tom yelled as we went through his gate.

"I won't."

But I wanted to save that for last. Sycamore Castle was a special place my mother had found. She'd shown it to Tom and me when we were toddlers, and we'd been playing there ever since.

"Turn left, Liz, we'll go to the log cabin first. It's there in the woods up ahead."

"A real log cabin?"

"Yeah. It's neat. It was there when my great-grandfather bought that woods, Daddy says."

"I'll race you," she called and was off like a jockey —a jockey in an unfamiliar western saddle anyway.

After we left the cabin, we rode through the woods till we got to the split-rail fence at the edge of the pasture. It was really pretty. The sun filtered through the trees and made dappled spots of light on the leaves and pine needles we were riding through. The chipmunks and squirrels were scurrying around everywhere. Getting ready for winter, I guess.

We were riding along slow, talking. I could see the fence up ahead. "Can you jump it?" I asked Liz.

She didn't even answer. She just took off. I let Prince have his head and just as we were sailing over, I heard a thud. I didn't even want to look back. I was sure Liz was lying back there, dead as a stick. I'd have to go before her dad to be sentenced for murder because it was all my fault. Just as I was imagining her beautiful blond hair all bloody and her teeth knocked out, Liz started to giggle. Finally I turned around. Cricket was just standing there like a lump. She had refused to take the fence, and Liz was on her hands and knees shaking leaves and pine needles out of her hair.

I jumped off Prince and hurdled the fence. "Oh, Liz! Are you okay? Did you break anything vital? That stupid Cricket. Plain lazy, that's all. She's jumped that fence a million times." I was furious at that stupid mare.

"No. I'm okay. I'm not used to that saddle, and when she stopped, I just went floating right over her head. But I landed on that soft stuff. Don't look so worried, Meg. We really have some times, don't we?"

Liz's calling me Meg made me think of Beeb right in the middle of our crisis. If it weren't for Pris, I'd really like to talk to Liz about him—what he had done at the concert and everything.

"You ride Prince now," I told her. "I'm going to teach that crazy Cricket a lesson." I don't believe in using a whip on animals, but if you don't show a horse who's boss, he'll run all over you. I picked up a stick and got on. Then I went back a few yards and rode her straight at that fence. This time she sailed over like a kite. Crazy ole cow. I didn't even have to use my switch. I patted her anyway. She was getting awfully old.

I showed Liz our fishing rock and the place where we swam in the summer when there'd been enough rain. Then we went to Sycamore Castle. Part of the root structure was exposed, and it made a terrace that hung out over the water. The trunk was so big that Mother, Tom, and I could all fit inside. We had nailed some boards on the outside so we could climb up to the branches.

Liz and I got off and turned the horses loose to eat grass. "It's like a fairy castle!" she said, and ran over to inspect it.

"Mother and I used to come down here and play we were princesses. She saved all the old curtains to use for our costumes. Once she rolled colored paper into a cone and sewed a big white tie-back curtain to it. I had a swell train."

Liz was lying on the terrace looking up at the clouds. "Your mother's really neat, you know that?"

"I know, but she's got Lizzie and . . . Daddy. I always wished I had a sister my age, or at least a girl friend close by. That was why I wanted to be a Hi Gal so bad."

"Well, I'm really glad you joined the club, but, gee, you've got Tom, and I think it's neat to have a *boy* for a friend."

"Tom's okay most of the time. He used to be better though."

"What happened?" Liz threw a stone in the creek. She looked so relaxed and happy. I can't tell you how glad I was to have a friend to talk to about important things.

"Well, Tom's always been spoiled. Being an only child, he's used to having his own way. I could usually handle that, but the last year it's been weird. He never was very smart in school. He's not retarded or anything, he's just more interested in cattle and farming and stuff than in books. But Liz, I swear, he's just not growing up. He's not interested in girls or anything. Do you know what I mean?"

"Sure. Sometimes I think boys are just slow. I've never liked a boy in my grade. Mike's a year and three months older than me."

"How old's Beeb?" That just popped out. Too late now.

"Fifteen in July, but Beeb's so shy, you'd never

know it. He's an orphan. Hey, why are you so interested in Beeb? Megan, do you like him?"

I was too embarrassed to look at her, but I couldn't
very well lie to someone I liked as much as Liz.

I rubbed a smooth ole root on Sycamore Castle for
luck. "Yes. Do you hate me?"

"Hate you? I think it's terrific. You'd be perfect together. Why should I hate you?"

"Pris."

"You sound as if you'd murdered her. I told you
about them. Beeb doesn't like her and never did give
her any reason to think he did. Honest. I mean, he
likes her okay. We've all been friends since Mrs.
Kelly's Nursery School, but she's not his girl friend.
We've just always stuck together, you know."

"But she likes him, and I took that vow . . . and I
really get jealous of her. I'm ashamed to admit it,
but I really do. She just seems to clutch on to him
like a leech. I feel guilty because of the way I feel
about Pris, but I just can't help it."

Liz leaned back against the bank. "I wouldn't worry
about Pris. I think she likes the idea of Beeb being
a big deal at school rather than really liking *him*.
Having people think she goes with Beeb Barber gives
her a lot of power, and you know how Pris can be a
real manipulator when she wants to. She and Beeb
are just so different, you know?"

"I don't know either one of them very well. I just
know I like him . . . a lot!"

"Pris's all spark and energy. My mother says,

'Brash, darling, really brash,' but Pris and I've been in the same gang for such a long time, I just accept her as she is, I guess. But she embarrasses Beeb sometimes. Beeb's sweet . . . gentle. He and Mike are like twins. I don't think they've ever even been angry at each other."

"Liz . . . he held my hand."

She leaned around and looked up at me. Did she ever seem surprised!

"At the concert when you were singing. Your lovely voice must have inspired him," I said, and grinned at her, even though I felt very self-conscious. She'd probably think I had no principles at all.

"Wow! Believe me, for Beeb that's practically a declaration of love."

I was really relieved by her reaction. But wouldn't you know it? Just when we were getting to the good part, Lizzie showed up. She was waving her arms as she ran down the hill. Then she fell flat on her face, of course.

"Is that Lizzie?"

You sure could tell Liz didn't have a pesty little sister. She seemed to think Lizzie's showing off was funny.

"We seem to have something besides our names in common. She can't stay on her feet any better than I can stay on Cricket."

I climbed out of the tree and went to get Lizzie. She went right up to Liz and said, "Megan said you were beautiful."

"I think *you*'re beautiful," Liz said, and won a friend. Lizzie's already beginning to show signs of being vain as a peacock.

"We might as well take her home," I said. "Mother's probably frantic looking for her, and we won't be able to get rid of her anyway."

I was going to put Lizzie up behind me on Cricket, but she insisted on riding with Liz.

When we got home, I decided Liz might as well see the whole catastrophe, so I took her with me to do my chores instead of giving her *Seventeen* to read, as I had originally planned. We even went into the chicken house to feed those disgusting chickens. When we got to the barn, Daddy was milking Harmony. He was pretty civilized while I introduced Liz, as much as anyone can be when he's sitting on a three-legged stool under an ole cow's belly, that is. But Lizzie was with us, of course, and she said, "Daddy, show Liz how you can give me a drink."

"Guests first, honey. Open your mouth, Liz."

I put my hands over my eyes. I was too mortified to watch. For a few awful moments I was certain he had wrecked the rest of my high school career. When I looked through my fingers, Liz had milk running down her chin, but she was laughing and puckering up her lips for more. Can you imagine aiming an ole cow's teat at Liz Ray? I wanted to kill myself.

"Liz, this here cow's named Harmony 'cause we needed some around here after Megan and Peaches declared war," said Daddy.

If he told that story, I'd run away from home.

"Who's Peaches?" Liz asked, as if she were really interested in some bad-tempered ole cow who had about killed me.

"This ole cow we had when Megan was little. Peaches took a dislike to Megan for some reason, went crazy every time Lucy brought her into the barn. Once she butted Megan off the partition there like she was a baseball."

"That's why Megan won't ever, ever learn to milk," Lizzie said, "but I can. Let me show her, Daddy."

But would you believe Liz even tried milking Harmony? I think milking is revolting. I finally dragged her away to help me pitch hay out of the loft for the horses. Daddy and Lizzie acted as if she had come to visit them. She was *my* guest, for heaven's sakes.

After we had tossed down several forkfuls, Liz flopped down in the hay because she thought it smelled so good. We lay there talking for a while, then Liz sat up so fast I thought she had a pain or something.

"Meg, I have a great idea! Let's have a Hi Gals hayride. You can ask Beeb."

Riding around in some prickly hay on a wagon didn't sound like such a good idea to me, but with Beeb . . . now, that was something else.

Mother invited Tom for supper, reminding me how nice he'd been about lending us Cricket. I knew she was right, but sometimes it's hard to be fair.

I swear Liz could talk anybody into anything.

Daddy said he'd fix a hayrack for us. Even said he'd let us use his Percheron team. Tom and I both almost dropped our teeth when he said that. Daddy's really proud of those horses. He even shows them at the state fair. She teased Tom, trying to get him to say he'd go with us, but even Liz can't accomplish miracles. When Tom Arnold asks a girl for a real date, the world'll slip off its axis. They finally worked out a compromise. He wouldn't ride in the hay wagon with us, but he agreed to drive the team.

Liz was probably able to work her magic on Daddy because she can sing. Mother told him about her singing "Tomorrow" at the concert. That made me feel guilty because I had been concentrating so much on Beeb, I couldn't even remember how it had sounded. After supper Mother got us all gathered around her new piano. I think she wanted to be sure Liz didn't miss it. Mother sings real well, and Daddy is always off-key, but with Liz's strong soprano they didn't sound bad. I just hoped they didn't sing "Danny Boy," 'cause then Daddy would get all sentimental and kiss Mother or something right in front of all of us. Liz's folks were so dignified. I didn't dare to imagine what she'd think.

After they'd sung about every song ever written, Mother closed the piano and laid her head on the top. Her face was all flushed, and she looked so happy. "Liz'll grow up to make records. Megan'll write smashing reviews for her in the newspaper. These kids are going to put Sagamon on the map, you know that, Joe?"

"And Lizzie'll be Miss America," he said. "You're a dreamer, you know that, Lucy Morgan?" I knew it was coming. Sure enough, he kissed her.

Maybe Liz didn't even notice much 'cause Lizzie put one hand on her hip, the other on her head, and started to wiggle around saying, "Here's Miss America." Ole square Lizzie in her pajamas with feet flashing a Miss America smile just cracked us all up.

When we finally got upstairs, I wanted to talk all night, but we were both exhausted. I thought Liz was asleep, but then she said it again, just like that night at her house.

"Gee, Megan, you're so lucky."

Wow! If she only knew. I was relieved she didn't think I was awful for liking Beeb when Pris did, but she'd never understand all the problems I had with the bus kids and everything. I always used to be able to rely on Tom, but now even that relationship was getting complicated. Thank goodness I had a girl friend . . . almost a best friend, I thought, looking over at Liz. She already seemed to be sleeping. Soon I was asleep too.

Twelve

* * * * * * * * * * * * * *

When Mike called the next morning to tell Liz he was coming out to pick her up, I got so excited I couldn't think straight. Would Beeb come with him? Of course, I felt as if I'd die if he didn't, but what would I do if he did? I decided I'd act like nothing had ever happened between us and give him the grand tour of the chicken house. Be cool, Megan, be cool.

When Mike's dad's car stopped by our gate, I could already see two crimson sweaters. Mother was coming back from the barn when they pulled up. She invited them in for a glass of milk and a few of her cinnamon buns. Of course they took her up on it.

After we had all sat down around the kitchen table, Liz and Mother chatted away as if Beeb and Mike were just nobody special at all. Thank heavens Lizzie was outside with Daddy.

"Mrs. Morgan, did Megan tell you the governor's going to hold a conference for young politicians?" Liz said. "Every district's going to elect a freshman or sophomore, like a leadership training thing, I guess."

"No, she didn't," Mother said. "I think that's a good

idea. I always think we could stand some sprucing up at party headquarters. Who's going to run?"

"We'll all work for Priscilla White." Liz made a sweeping gesture around the table that included Mike, Beeb, and *me*.

"I heard those country kids are going to put up a candidate," Mike said to Liz.

"Those country kids," indeed. Where did he think he was right now? Paris, France?

"There's more of them. They might even be able to give Pris a run for her money." It was as if Mike had read my mind. I'd always thought that if us bus kids got ourselves organized, we could run that school just by sheer numbers alone. Listening to Mike's smug remarks, I wished even more that we had. I'd wanted to be a Hi Gal more than anything, but I hadn't counted on it meaning I'd have to help the worst excuse for a leader at Sagamon get elected. I gave Mother a see-what-I-mean look, and she winked at me. At least now she'd understand when I tried to explain to her what the town kids' attitude was toward us, but that was small consolation.

"They haven't got a chance. We've got Megan's column," Liz answered, just as cocky as you please, as if I'd already endorsed Pris in "Megan's Beat." Suddenly my stomach hurt. I didn't even want to think about the governor's conference. I wanted to think about Beeb and the hayride. How was I ever going to get up the nerve to ask him to go with me?

"Excuse me a minute," I said, rather calmly I thought. But the moment I got up and headed for the stairs, I realized they would all think I had to go to the bathroom. I'm such a klutz. What I really did was tear up the stairs and call Tom.

"What would you think of a girl who asked you for a date, I mean now that we've got women's lib and everything? . . . Of course I'm not kidding. . . . *Why* would you think she was too aggressive? . . . Oh, what do *you* know, Tom Arnold? . . . I'll bring Cricket home this afternoon. . . . What conference? . . . Oh, *that* thing! Not you too. . . . I know I'm always trying to get you involved with school, but the conference wasn't exactly what I had in mind. . . . Look, I don't have time to talk about it now. I've got company. This afternoon, okay? See you."

When I went back to the kitchen, everyone had finished, and Liz said, "Megan, let's show the guys our horses." That was a good idea as far as I was concerned. I sure was too antsy to sit.

Liz grabbed Mike's hand and pulled him along as she showed him everything from that ugly old sow Bertha to Harmony. Beeb was smiling his usual sweet smile, and he walked with me, but wasn't much help with the conversation. Or maybe I was babbling and not giving him a chance. I was so nervous, I was perspiring in fifty-degree weather.

Lizzie had been feeding the pigs, but she joined us when he was finally beginning to talk. I could have throttled her.

Beeb said, "Your mother sure is pretty, Meg."

"Everybody says Megan looks just like her," Lizzie said as she skipped along *between* us. "I look like Daddy."

Beeb looked right at me and said, "You do look like her." Then he blushed and looked down at his running shoes, and patted Lizzie's curls. She ran ahead to catch up with Liz, thank heavens.

I wanted to yell out loud for the whole world to hear, "Beeb Barber thinks I'm pretty!" but I guess that would sound pretty silly. I was still trying to decide about asking him to the hayride. Tom was probably right. I probably shouldn't ask him to anything until he had asked me out at least once. I'd play it cool. Daddy's always saying I'm pushy and impatient. I sure don't want Beeb to think I'm aggressive. Then it was as if I couldn't control it. The words just popped out. What did Tom and Daddy know anyway?

"Would you like to go on a Hi Gals hayride with me?" I asked, too fast, without a trace of grace or charm.

The moment I'd said it, I felt miserable. My whole reputation ruined at thirteen. Branded forever as a brazen hussy.

"A hayride? That sounds great. I'd really like to. When is it?"

He said yes. He said yes. He said yes! I felt like dancing. Cripes! What was Pris going to do? She'd kill me . . . shun me . . . get me kicked out of the club. Why had I done it? Would have been better never to have gotten in with these kids at all than to be dropped.

"Uh . . . I don't know. Liz and I just planned it yesterday, Daddy's going to let us use his Percherons. . . . Tom's going to drive . . . but we haven't talked to the other girls yet. I'll tell you in English class when I find out. Okay?"

"Swell. Uh, maybe we should . . . uh, get to know each other a little better before the party. Maybe you could stay with Liz again . . . only not disappear this time. What happened to you guys at the carnival that night?"

"Well, we had to . . . uh . . . well, if you want to know the truth, I got really sick." I couldn't seem to keep my mouth shut. I'm such a dummy.

"Those rides always make me sick too. I was *so* glad you and Liz didn't suggest that Mike and me go with you on any of them that night."

"You were?"

"Yeah. Guess I'm prone to motion sickness. I can't even ride on the back of the bus when we go to an out-of-town game." He grinned, but looked kind of like he was ashamed. "Coach knows, but I don't tell any of the team . . . except Mike."

"You can't imagine how humiliated I was at the carnival. It was the first time I'd ever slept over at Liz's house and all . . . and you mustn't tell her, but her dad really gives me the willies."

"I know what you mean. Even Mike tries to steer clear of Judge Ray. He'd make a good commanding general. But I was really disappointed that night when you and Liz didn't show up."

"I was so mad at myself . . . those awful taffy apples didn't help a bit."

"If I promise to keep you away from taffy apples and Tilt-A-whirls, will you stay in town some night next week? Maybe we could go to the movies or get a Coke or something. Dig up stuff for your scandal sheet. . . ."

Who's afraid of Priscilla White anyway? I can take anything she can dish out . . . maybe. It's not like they were going steady or anything. "What do you mean, scandal sheet? I'll have you know I only report the facts . . . mostly."

All of a sudden I thought of a story I'd wanted to put in a column . . . well, actually, I'd just wanted to know, but the column was a good excuse. "How did you get your nickname? That should make a good piece for 'Megan's Beat.' "

He flushed and looked uncomfortable. I was sorry I'd asked, but it was too late.

"My aunt used to call me Bill, but when I was little I couldn't pronounce it. What I said sounded more like Beeb, I guess."

"I promise I won't put it in my column," I said.

I was really glad when Liz called to us then, because I could tell he was embarrassed.

"Megan, could we saddle the horses? I want to show Mike how I can ride a western saddle just like a cowboy." Liz was leading Prince out of the barn.

"Did she really almost get killed yesterday when this treacherous animal refused to take the fence?" Mike asked, and ruffled Liz's hair.

"You're lucky she's alive. Almost broke her neck." I winked at Liz.

"Megan's the cowgirl. She got him to jump the stupid fence. You guys should see her ride." Liz was such a good friend.

"Why don't we show the cowgirl the big city life?" Beeb said, and I felt so happy I wanted to turn a million cartwheels. "Maybe she could stay in town Wednesday night? Mike and I could pick you both up after Hi Gals." He didn't sound so shy.

"Good idea. Spend the night with me, Meg," Liz said.

Well, at least if Pris tried to kill me, I'd be close to the hospital, I told myself.

After they'd left, I went out to the barn with Daddy for a while, but he made me so angry I didn't stay long.

"Is that red-headed Barber boy the one Lucy tells me you've got a crush on?"

"He just asked me for a date. I guess it's not so one-sided as you seem to think."

Daddy just threw back his head and laughed like I'd told him a joke.

"What's so funny?"

"He's kind of quiet for you, isn't he?" Daddy said.

"He's not so shy. I can get him to talk."

"Oh, now I'm sure you can, Megan. You'll lead that poor boy a merry chase, I'd bet. If I had the conscience the good Lord intended me to, I probably should warn him."

I don't know who'll drive me to the loony bin first, Daddy or Tom.

"Daddy! I'll have you know he's captain of the basketball team and *very* popular up at the high school. You should be proud that he asked me out."

"Oh, now Megan, I am. I am. He seems like a nice enough boy. Just wonderin' if he can keep up with you and if you won't tire of him soon as you have him marching around like you did those boys over at Heckathorne."

Fathers can be so dense. He just didn't seem to understand how different this was.

That afternoon I rode Cricket home. Kitty had written me a letter, and I should have answered it, but I decided to wait until after the hayride, when I might have something really exciting to tell her. Riding over to Tom's I had a brilliant idea, but he adamantly refused to cooperate. I thought if he would ask Pris to the movies or something, it might distract her from thinking about me and Beeb. Actually I think Tom enjoyed seeing me stew. Some friend.

We spent the afternoon clipping Rudy's hooves.

It was time for me to do my chores and Tom was driving me across the field when he made the roof of the world fall in on me.

"Some of the guys in ag are trying to get me to run for that governor's conference," Tom said, and looked straight ahead, as if he were driving in heavy traffic on the Los Angeles freeway.

I just remembered he had mentioned something about the conference on the phone that morning, but I'd been too preoccupied to really listen.

"Don't you dare!" I screeched. He *knew* Pris was running. "Don't you realize I've got enough problems with the Hi Gals putting the heat on me to back Pris of all people? You just can't do this to me!"

"You know, you're really selfish, Megan!" he said, and gave me the dirtiest look you could ever imagine. "All you've been preaching about since we started high school is 'get involved.' 'Get involved,' 'go out for sports,' 'join the band.' But when I start to think about something that isn't your idea, you get all bent outta shape."

He stopped the pickup at our gate. I got out but held on to the door. "Please don't run, Tom." He wouldn't even turn his head, just sat there looking as stubborn as Ethel. I slammed the door, and Tom whirled the truck around and left me standing there in his dust.

Thirteen

* * * * * * * * * * * * * *

Monday is never my favorite day of the week, but with Tom sore at me and thinking of running for the governor's conference plus the Hi Gals' beginning to let me know, not very subtly, that it was time for me to come out for Pris in "Megan's Beat," I had a miserable day.

The nightmare began in biology class. This girl named Suzy Lane came over before class to tell me about a picnic she and her sister had had for their friends over the weekend. Her sister was wearing new jeans, and while they were fooling around the inside seam of her jeans had split all the way around, and she hadn't been wearing any underwear. Suzy wanted me to put it in "Megan's Beat." While she was talking, and I was writing and trying to think how I could clean it up, Pris bounced by and hit my arm. On purpose.

She opened her eyes wide, planted a phony angelic expression on her face, and said, "Whoops! Sorry, Megan, I didn't mean to mess up what you were writing. Of course, it was like Liz and I were saying yesterday afternoon, you don't seem to be writing about the important issues anyway." She went swishing on back to her seat.

Suzy said, "What's her trouble?"

I looked back to where Liz was sitting, and she mouthed, "I told her about Beeb."

"Beats me," I said to Suzy, and crossed my fingers. "Now where did you say this happened?"

Biology class was only a warning. I really knew things were getting serious when I went to *The Sentinel* office to turn in my copy, and Mr. Finley motioned for me to come into his office. I could just smell trouble. I should've known that the reason Pris was so persuasive with everyone was because she knew how to use all of the ammunition she had.

Ruby Lacey has worked for Mr. Finley for years, so he must know all of her tricks. She started filing in the cabinet right outside his door, so he kicked it shut. "Ruby's curiosity sometimes makes her a good reporter and sometimes just makes her darn nosy," he said and smiled. I wished I knew how to deal with Pris as easily.

Mr. Finley tilted back in his swivel chair and read each page of my column very carefully He didn't usually do that, and I got all tensed up. When he finished the last page, he looked over the top of his half-glasses and said, "Megan, you're improving all the time. Really getting the feel of it. Still enjoying it?"

"Yes, sir. Well, most of the time, except when somebody gets mad over nothing . . . when I didn't mean any harm." I knew he hadn't asked me into his office to discuss my writing style, and I wished he would just tell me what was on his mind. Recently it seemed like everyone had some sinister warning for me.

"I don't want to upset you, but it's like I told you when you started, you can't please everybody. That's why I thought maybe I better show you this." He handed me a note someone had typed, so they couldn't be identified, I guess.

Dear Mr. Finley,

All the kids at SHS think the new column is a super idea, and we're really glad you thought of starting it. But the current writer, who doesn't even live in Sagamon, just doesn't seem to know enough about the school to pick up the really important events. In fact some of the items are really hokey. There are so many more qualified writers who are better acquainted with the leaders of the school that a number of us think it would be a good idea to consider a replacement. Especially if the present reporter doesn't begin to better cover the real news.

SHS Concerned Students

"Whose feathers did you ruffle this week? Got any idea?"

I examined Mr. Finley's floor for a while, trying to decide what to do. Telling him Pris probably wrote it was being a ratfink, but not telling him was like letting a criminal go unidentified. Life just seems to get more complicated every day.

Finally I decided Pris wasn't really playing fair herself. I didn't exactly expect her to pat me on the back for not supporting her candidacy and taking Beeb away from her, but it seemed to me she was hitting below the belt. Anyway, I decided good leaders weren't sneaky.

"Pris White would like to cut out my gizzard."

"Why?"

"I asked a boy she likes to go to a party with me, and I'm not sure I want to endorse her for something in my column. Is that enough to get me fired?" *Cripes, fired from my first job at thirteen! At this rate I'll be in the penitentiary before I'm twenty-one.*

"Oh, I reckon not. I never have paid much attention to anyone's complaints when they didn't have guts enough to sign a name."

"Thanks, Mr. Finley. I keep trying to avoid the minefields, but I don't seem to be very good at it. Sorry I cause you so many headaches."

I had my hand on the doorknob when Mr. Finley said, "Did the boy say yes?"

That made me laugh. For a moment he made me forget about Tom and having to face the conference talk at lunch next period. "He sure did!" I said.

Walking back to school, I couldn't decide what I dreaded most—lunch, the Hi Gal meeting, or Tom's deep-freeze treatment on the bus. Here I had a date with the handsomest boy, the best basketball player in the whole school, my first date, for Pete's sakes, and I couldn't even think about it without almost getting an ulcer. Why did Pris have to be a Hi Gal anyway? When those girls saw Beeb come to pick me up at the next meeting, there'd be no way I'd ever convince them that the reason I wasn't backing Pris was because I thought she'd be a rotten leader.

On Wednesday night I marched off to that Hi Gal meeting like a soldier going into battle. The meeting was being held in Mickey's family room. Liz and Pris were already there holding court.

"You guys, you aren't going to believe what happened. I'm so excited, I could just die!" Pris was saying as we walked in.

She had her arms folded across her chest and was rocking and swaying as if a band were accompanying her performance.

"I had all this work to do, so I stayed after school to catch up. I was coming out just as basketball practice was over, and I just happened to run into Bud Adams. Guess I never had really noticed before how good-looking he is. I mean my heart about stopped when I looked at him, all sparkly clean from the shower . . . all those muscles rippling under that letter sweater. . . ."

I had to hand it to her. She had everyone sitting on the edge of their seats just hanging on her every word.

"Well, when he asked if he could walk me home, so confident and sure of himself, I almost had a heart attack. I like a guy who's aggressive, don't you? I mean shy guys are such a bore!"

And there's no better judge of boring than Pris, I

was thinking when Liz punched me in the ribs. I had to put my hand over my mouth to keep from laughing out loud.

"Did he ask you for a date?" Mickey asked, sounding excited.

"Well, of course, but I told him we had Hi Gal meeting tonight. I mean, I think it's not being very loyal to the club to run out early to meet a boy when we have important business to discuss. You know what I mean?"

Everybody but Liz and me nodded their heads like robots.

"I did tell him though that we were having a party . . . that silly hayride you've been talking about, Liz, and he said he'd just love to go. Thought it would be quaint."

No wonder so many of the Hi Gals went out for the Thespian Club. Those girls can switch roles faster'n I can change my jeans, but Pris was the worst. After the meeting had come to order, we planned the hayride—picked a date, decided on refreshments, all that stuff.

When Jane said, "Megan, who are you going to ask? Tom?" my voice cracked, but I managed to explain for about the ninetieth time that Tom was my friend, not my boyfriend.

"I'm taking . . . well, I think, I'm taking . . . uh, Beeb Barber."

Ten mouths dropped open in unison. Liz started to say something, but Pris interrupted her. "Isn't that terrific? I suggested to Beeb when I told him I *just* couldn't go out with him anymore—that he should find someone younger, less sophisticated."

Talk about saving face! Priscilla's all of four months older than I am. The silence lasted about five seconds, and then everyone started screaming and squealing and hugging me. It wasn't long before everyone was talking about Pris and Bud, Megan and Beeb, just like that was the way it had always been.

I was just beginning to feel more relaxed when Jane changed the subject to Pris's running for the governor's conference.

"Who's your competition?" Mickey asked.

"Of course no one's going to say until they get the nomination, but I hear the sophomores are going to put up Donnie Nash," Pris said.

"He'll be easy to beat," Liz said.

"I've heard the bus kids are going to put up a candidate," Jane said. "If they all stick together, we've got problems. Have you heard anything about that, Megan?"

"There's been some discussion, but I don't think anyone has decided for sure," I said, grateful that Tom's name hadn't surfaced and vowing that by tomorrow night I would have him talked out of it.

"Look, I keep telling you we have nothing to worry about. Megan'll swing the fringe vote with her column, and that'll make Pris a shoo-in," Liz said. I just couldn't believe it, coming from her of all people. *She* knew how I felt about Pris. If she was aware that

Tom was thinking about entering the race, she didn't say so, but I felt as if everyone in the room were waiting for me to lead a cheer for Pris. The tension was so thick you could cut it with a knife.

By the time the guys picked Liz and me up, I was really a wreck. I just couldn't figure out how getting the two things I wanted so much—to be a Hi Gal and to go out on a date with Beeb—could have gotten me into such a mess. I'm sure that when we left Pris was putting a hex on me. What if I blew it the first time, and Beeb never wanted to see me again? His being a sophomore, a basketball star, and more experienced made me kind of nervous. He must *never* know this was my first date. I was really glad Liz and Mike would be with us, you know, to keep the conversation going and everything.

Mike didn't have his dad's car, so we walked to the Toot 'N' Tell'um, this place where all the kids go. Now you'd think almost anyone could walk down the sidewalk next to a boy, but not me. I kept bumping into him. I mean I was mortified. He probably thought I was being suggestive or something, because I was moving like a drunk who couldn't walk a straight line. Then he put his arm around my waist. I couldn't tell if he did it because he felt like it or to keep from getting battered black and blue. Anyway, I really liked it. He was so tall!

We all ordered hamburgers, french fries, and Cokes. Mickey's mother had only served us dip and chips, and I was really hungry. I had just taken my first bite when Mike said, "I suppose you guys planned Pris's campaign tonight, didn't you?" He pointed his finger at Liz, but he grinned when he said, "Before you make plans for me and Beeb to run all over town getting supplies and stuff, I hope you'll keep in mind that Coach likes to see us show up for practice now and then. Right, Beeb?"

"Remember last year's talent show!" Beeb slapped his hand across his forehead. "They kept us so busy, I forgot my locker number the few times I made it to the gym."

Suddenly I felt queasy. If they'd just talk about anything but how they all work together like one mean machine, I thought I'd probably be okay. But I guess what was really bothering me was Liz's attitude. How could she act as if there were no question about my supporting Pris? Did *she* really think Pris would make a good leader? I couldn't understand her.

After that the conversation turned to the hayride and basketball, so I began to feel better. When we started walking home, Mike and Beeb were sort of bantering with each other, and then Liz challenged Mike to a race. I think she probably did it so Beeb and I could talk. At first I couldn't decide if I was glad or not, but trying to make conversation at least kept my mind off Tom and that stupid conference.

"I'm really glad you asked me to the hayride," Beeb said, and I wished I could record it to play it back to Tom. "I'd been trying to work up enough courage to call you since the carnival."

"You had? That's funny. You don't know how scared I was to ask you. I thought you might think I was forward. Or that you wouldn't want to go or something."

"I noticed you the first day in English class. Liked your braid." He took hold of it and sort of stroked it. I felt like I'd die. And to think I'd once thought about cutting it off.

"I know they say it's okay now for girls to ask boys, but I felt funny because . . . well, if you want to know the truth, I've never had a real date before."

He laughed but sounded sort of embarrassed. "Tonight's the first time I ever asked anyone out myself."

"But . . . Pris?" Now why did I have to mention her? I'm such a dummy.

"I know what everybody always thought, but I never really called her or anything. Mike and Liz would always sort of set things up, you know. I was afraid you'd think we were really tight. That's why I held your hand at the concert. Did that make you mad? Liz had mentioned that you and Tom were just friends, not dating or anything."

"I was glad you did." I swear I'm going to put a muffler on my mouth. I really am. When we get to Liz's house, I want him to kiss me good night. I know I'll let him if he tries, and then he'll know for sure I'm a hussy.

As it turned out, he didn't have any reason to think I was. But not because I suddenly developed strength of character. Liz and Mike were waiting for us at the corner of her block, catching their breath. We walked up toward Liz's house together, but were only halfway up the steps when the porch light flashed on. I don't know why, but I felt as if I'd been caught shoplifting or something. Judge Ray was at the door checking his watch.

"Elizabeth, it is ten thirty. Tell your friends good night."

For just a moment I thought he meant me too, and I had visions of sleeping in the park. But Liz didn't even seem surprised. "Good night, you guys," she said just as calm as you please. "Come on, Megan. I want to play my new record for you."

I don't know why, but when I said good night to Beeb, I whispered.

Fourteen

* * * * * * * * * * * * * * *

I found out the next day at lunch that Pris was going
to make planning the hayride as difficult as possible
for me. She started out by making some snotty remarks that really hurt my feelings.

"I don't know why we ever planned to go way out
in the sticks to ride around on some smelly old pile
of hay," she said. "Bud and I think it lacks class."
Translated that meant they didn't have a ride.
Mickey's dad had a station wagon, so we finally worked
it out for Pris and Bud to come out with them. And
when Mickey asked who was going to drive us around,
I decided the whole idea had been a mistake. Liz
was the one who said Tom was driving. It was getting
to the point that I got uneasy every time his name
came up in one of our conversations.

"I heard this morning that he's the one the bus
kids are going to run against me for the conference!"
Pris shrieked. "We won't have any fun at all if *he*'s
there. I mean, we'd have to watch what we said about
the campaign and everything."

"Megan can handle Tom," Liz said, and I wondered what she meant by that.

"And he hasn't decided to run for sure yet," I said, more for my benefit than theirs.

Tom wasn't on the bus that night. I thought I had seen the Arnolds' car going around the corner when I came out of the school. Mother told me when I got home that Ethel's mother wasn't well, so they'd gone to visit her in Champaign for a few days. We were going to do their chores, so that meant until Sunday dumb ole Rudy was in my care.

I spent the weekend getting ready for the hayride. Daddy said if he had known having a hayride would have turned me into such a good worker, he would have taken my class all over the county every year. I curried those Percherons till I was almost down to the skin. Then I started waxing the harness and polishing the brass. It was a lot of work. I kept wishing Tom were home to help. No matter how long it took me, I wasn't going to give Pris a chance to say our equipment was trashy. I smelled and smelled the hay, and it seemed okay to me. I did suggest to Mother that just to be on the safe side we might spray some air freshener on it, but she thought that was going too far.

Monday morning Tom was on the bus, but when I got on, he was sitting with Tim and entertaining everybody with crazy stories about his trip, half of which I bet he'd made up. Since I couldn't talk to him, I just kept thinking about Friday night and the hayride, and that made me feel good, except I sat with Betty Sue and I kept wishing I could ask her to come.

I hadn't realized that when you made new friends, you had to give up the ones you had. It just didn't seem fair.

About a million kids were gathered around the bulletin board when I tried to get down the hall to my locker. Liz was up front, but when she saw me, she managed to worm her way through the crowd to tell me what was posted.

"Cheerleading tryouts are a week from Friday, can you believe it? I thought we would have lots more time. Megan, you've got to go out with Mickey and me." Liz was really excited. She grabbed my shoulders and almost shook my head off. "Won't it be terrific? We'll get to go to out-of-town games on the bus with the team."

"But why me? You guys were cheerleaders in junior high. I've never—" Even though I'd tried to talk Tom into going out for cheerleading, I'd only been half-serious. Guess I knew he wouldn't want to do it.

"You're the only one," Liz went on. "Mickey and I talked about it this weekend. Donna Mabry cheered with us at Central, but she moved away last summer. You're athletic, and we can show you the routines. Think how much fun it'll be now that you're going with Beeb!"

"I know, but won't some of the other Hi Gals, like maybe Pris, want to try out?"

"No, believe me. We went all through this in junior high. Everybody is doing something else except Jane, and she's too shy. Pris is a klutz in the gym. She couldn't do the splits if she had elastic legs. But she'll get us elected. You know how persuasive she is. With her on our side we can't lose. Say you'll do it, Meg!"

Trying to imagine Pris on my side was hard, but I said, "If you think you and Mickey can teach me the routines, I'd love to, but I bet we'll have tons of competition. I never saw so many kids clustered around the bulletin board."

"The Governor's Leadership Conference is up there too. They finally anounced it officially. The candidates have to declare next week. Listen, we've got to start practicing right away. When do you have a free period?"

Learning what Mickey and Liz had been doing for two years wasn't as easy as Liz had made it sound, so I called Mother during ninth period, and she said I could practice on campus after school and then stay over at Mickey's house. Liz had to be home for dinner at seven o'clock, no matter what, so we stopped at six thirty and made plans to have another session after dinner in Mickey's basement. We were just leaving school when basketball practice let out, so Beeb and Mike walked most of the way home with us. It was just the way I always dreamed it would be, and Beeb thought it was terrific that I was going out for cheerleading. We'd get to see each other lots more if I were on the squad. I could just see us singing on the bus after we had won an out-of-town game, Beeb holding my hand on the sly so that Coach wouldn't notice.

I didn't think I could wait till the hayride. To tell you the truth, I've never been to many parties, you know, without parents. In the country we all live so far away from each other that our folks have to take us, so usually they just stay too. You can imagine how much fun that is. I felt as if I were just beginning to be alive.

That night I couldn't go to sleep, even though Mickey and I had really worn ourselves out practicing. I was too nervous and keyed up. Beeb had said one reason he was glad about the hayride was that the guys could get to know his girl that way. I would be totally ecstatic about being Beeb Barber's girl if it weren't for Pris—I know she still likes him. You can just tell about things like that. She pretends she's crazy about Bud now, but I see her watching Beeb in class and stuff, and she still really treats me mean every chance she gets.

But I try not to let Pris bother me *too* much, because I'm really beginning to feel that Liz and Mickey are almost my best friends. I know they've all been together for a long time like Tom and me, but it's building. I can feel it. This summer Beeb will have his license, so I'll get into town more. And Liz wants me to go to camp with her for three weeks. I've never been to camp, but I'll try anything once. Of course, Daddy thinks it's pretty stupid to spend four hundred and fifty dollars to go sleep in a tent in the woods. He told Mother he'd string up a tarp out back in our woods if I was that eager to get eaten alive by chiggers. He just doesn't understand that sharing something like a camp experience would really help me to be good friends with Liz. The only problem is, Liz's camp is scheduled at the same time we usually enter our 4-H projects at the state fair. Betty Sue reminded me about that on the bus this morning. She also said she thought it would be pretty crummy if I didn't enter this year, since I'd practically twisted everybody's arms off to get them to compete in the first place.

I can't understand why things have to get so complicated. To build a friendship, you've got to share a lot, work on things, and have funny, stupid times together. Even though I sometimes feel as if I'm being pulled in two directions, I just know I'm going to make it with Liz and Mickey and Beeb and those kids, and I also know I'm going to do it without letting Pris dance me around on a string like she tries to do with everyone else. But I can't let the Heckathorne kids down either. Cripes, why couldn't my life be simple? Finally, I fell asleep, even though my left leg felt as if I might be getting a charley horse from doing the splits.

Tuesday afternoon when I got on the bus, I still had hopes of talking Tom out of declaring his candidacy. But we had practiced cheerleading so hard, my muscles felt like rubber, and I had enough homework to discourage Einstein, so I just slumped in the first empty seat and didn't even look for Tom. Slowly I began to realize it was incredibly quiet. When I'd gotten on, there had been the usual roar, maybe even louder than usual. Now no one was saying anything. When I turned around, everyone looked as if they had been caught doing something dirty. How could I have offended them this time? They had been kind of standoffish recently, but today was different. Something was up. I thought hard as we covered those seven miles, and I was stumped. When we stopped at our lane, Tom said, "Hey, Megan, wait up." It was the first thing he'd said to me the whole trip.

I stopped on the bus step and looked back. Everybody but Tom seemed to be frozen in place, all watching me. He was climbing over legs, books, and lunch buckets and evidently was going to get off with me.

"Okay, Thomas Archibald Arnold, what was going on in there?" I said as the bus pulled away.

In thirteen years I thought I had seen Tom in every possible mood, but I was wrong. I'd never seen him embarrassed before. I'd always thought Tom was too spoiled ever to let anything embarrass him.

"I told those guys you wouldn't do it, but they made me ask you anyway," he said, but didn't look at me.

"What guys? Do what?"

"Well, the kids on our bus . . . the kids on all the buses actually . . . we've been talking about how it's time some of us had a little say around that lousy school, and—"

"Tom! You told me that Sunday. I agree. I just don't want *you* to—"

"They would have picked you. We all know you'd

be the best candidate, but what we really need is for you to use your column, and they didn't think you'd run against your snooty friend anyway, so they picked me, and . . . you think my running's a joke, don't you? I told 'em—"

"Tom, will you just hush for a minute. I can't make heads or tails of what you're saying." But I could smell trouble. "Of course, I don't think your running is a joke. Lord knows I've been wishing you guys would get involved from the first day. That's not why I asked you not to run. With Pris running, it just makes things so awkward." I looked at him real hard. "You kids didn't really think if it came to that, I wouldn't vote for you, did you? You just couldn't have."

"I need more than your vote. While you've been jumping around waving pom-poms the whole school's been getting heated up about this leadership thing."

Tom watched the toe of his sneaker digging up our yard while he said, "The way everybody's got it figured, some of the kids who go to that thing are going to be running for office in a few years, making up laws and stuff. Maybe even be senator or governor of the whole state. We might as well let 'em know farmers have something to say."

"Tom, you *know* I think it's about time those politicians found out there's a place right outside Chicago and it's called Illinois, but that's not the point! I'm not sure I can use my column to get *anyone* elected. That's not democratic." I'd been thinking about it and was planning to tell Pris. It was a good try anyway.

"Shoot. You think ole man Finley doesn't use *The Sentinel* to get Democrats elected around here?" He dropped his eyes again. "Anyway, there's something else I want you to do for me."

This was beginning to feel like slow torture.

"*Sometimes* you know how to use your head. Me and the rest of the kids thought you could be my campaign manager, write fancy speeches, plan our strategy and stuff, but I told them you probably wouldn't work against your highbrow friend."

"Your *campaign manager?*" I screamed. I felt as if he'd hit me in the stomach with his fist. "Oh, no!"

"Megan, I've got to have one. Pris White said after school today that she was going to ask Liz Ray to be hers."

Well, that settled it! "I won't do it! And you're mean and cruel even to ask me!"

Tom turned on his heel and stalked away. "I knew you wouldn't. You're too high society now!" he yelled at me, and started running across the field.

"And you're as lowdown as a snake, Tom Arnold!" I yelled back.

When I went in the house, Mother asked me what Tom and I were screaming about and why I didn't drive him home. I told her and then went up to my room and cried till Daddy finally made me go do my chores. All the time I was feeding the animals I kept thinking about Tom. He had some nerve asking me to be his campaign manager. Wasn't it enough that he was running against Pris? I wanted to die! He could just get someone else. How could he expect me to ruin my life?

At supper Mother tried to take my mind off Tom by talking about what I should wear to the hayride. She worried about me being warm, and I worried about being beautiful. But I guess it didn't really matter. The hayride would probably be my last date with Beeb anyway. Now that Liz was Pris's campaign manager, she and Mike sure weren't going to double with us if I didn't support Pris, so I wouldn't be able to stay at Liz's house, and Beeb didn't have his license. Maybe he wouldn't even want to see me anymore anyway. I just couldn't bear thinking about that.

As if I didn't have enough problems, Lizzie had to put her two cents in.

"What am I going to wear, Mommie?" she asked.

"You're not going!" I didn't really mean to scream, but there was no reason for her to carry on like I'd stabbed her either.

Of course Daddy *would* take her side. There are just so many things Daddy doesn't understand at all.

"I don't see what it would hurt for her to ride along, Megan," he said, and patted her shoulder. She'd put her head down on the table and was crying like I'd killed her. "She won't take up much room."

Mother got up and went into the pantry. When she got in there, she said, "Joe, I can't reach this can, will you come and help me, please."

"What can? We're almost finished—"

"*Joe,* would you just come here." Mother sounded a little bit exasperated.

Lizzie still had her head down on the table and kept bellowing, except when she raised it up to say, "Mean ole selfish Megan!" But I could hear Mother and Daddy whispering. Daddy said, "But, Lucy, she's only thirteen, for crying out loud."

Lizzie let out another wail, so I couldn't hear Mother, but then Daddy said, "But that was different, we were older."

He didn't sound so mad, and when they came back to the table, I knew Mother had fixed it.

"Lizzie," she said, "Friday you and I are going to have a party just for you. When we go to town to sell the eggs, we'll stop at Aunt Betty's and pick up Timmie and Martha and take them to Kramer's for chocolate sodas. How about that?"

"I want strawberry."

"Okay. Strawberry."

"And dumb ole Megan can't come?"

"Don't call your sister names. No, Megan has to go to school. This will be just our party."

Lizzie put a thumb in each side of her mouth and made the most hideous face at me you've ever seen. Can you imagine how humiliating it would have been to have had my little sister on that hayride? I mean, she'd be even more inhibiting than Judge Ray's porch light.

Mother stopped by my room like she always does

to say good night, but even though I knew she meant well, I wasn't in any mood to talk like we sometimes do.

"I know this is a hard decision for you, honey, but you and Tom have been through a lot together. You've shared your whole lives."

"Well, we won't anymore, because I'm not going to do it! He can just get some of those other kids to run his campaign. . . ."

"Who would you suggest?"

I put my chin in my hands and said, "That's the problem. I've been trying to think of someone who'd really be good. What's so awful about all of this is I really want him to beat the socks off Pris. I mean she's a manipulator, not a leader. But why do I have to give up Liz and Beeb and everybody just because Tom suddenly decides to go into politics?"

"If they're really your friends, they surely wouldn't even expect you to work against Tom, would they?"

"Sometimes I think those kids've got tunnel vision. You remember the day Mike was out here and he put country kids down right in front of us?"

"They seem to have accepted you, and you're a country kid."

"But it's like . . . like they expect me to forget who I am and just slap a coat of paint over the old me so I'll look just like them." I put my head down on my desk. "This isn't the way I thought it would be at all. I thought I'd make the breakthrough, and then they'd like Tom, Tim, Betty Sue, all of us. Instead they expect me to close the gate right in my old friends' faces. But the bus kids aren't any better—"

"Megan, I can't understand a thing you're saying with your head buried like that."

"It doesn't make any sense anyway. I just said nobody's attitude has changed one bit!"

Every night before I went to sleep, I'd been writing in my notebook my fantasies of the way the hayride would turn out. I was putting down stuff I'd never be able to report in "Megan's Beat." Those pages could have sold to *Playgirl*. But the truth was, Beeb hadn't even kissed me yet, for Pete's sakes. When Mother left, I threw my notebook against the wall and pulled the quilt over my head.

Fifteen

* * * * * * * * * * * * * *

I read my history on the bus the next morning. Tom and I weren't speaking, and no one else said anything to me either. We were all stiff as sticks with each other. I knew Tom must have told everyone before I got on that I wasn't going to be his campaign manager.

At lunchtime I was starting toward our table with my tray, and I almost dropped it. Pris was jumping around like always, but everyone was in an uproar, and they were all talking to Liz.

"Hey, Megan, isn't the election going to be a blast?" Mickey said as I scooted in. "Liz's going to be Pris's campaign manager! The candidates don't announce who their managers are until next week, but we're going to start making posters at Hi Gal meeting next Wednesday."

I nodded and got interested in my sloppy joe.

"Pris, with the Hi Gals behind you none of those other creeps've got a chance," Jane said, rather smugly, I thought.

"Look, you guys, everybody's really got to pitch in," Liz said. I took a bite of my sandwich but I couldn't seem to swallow. "My grades, especially Latin, are horrendous, and we've got cheerleading tryouts. This'll be a test of your loyalty. If we're going to win this election, I'm going to need tons of help on the campaign. No copping out."

"Hi Gals never lose elections!" Pris said, and banged the table.

While they all talked at once about campaign ideas I tuned them out and looked around the cafeteria. Across the aisle I saw a girl with curls that reminded me of Lizzie's. She was sitting by herself and pretending to be very interested in a paperback book she had in front of her. It looked as if her face hurt. I knew just how she felt.

Lunch seemed to last about five hours, but the bell finally rang, and I was thinking so hard, I forgot we had cheerleading practice.

Liz yelled at me, "Hey, Meg, wait up. We've gotta practice."

When we were sitting on a bench putting on our sneakers, and no one else was around, I decided I better talk to her. I was even giving myself this big pep talk about how Liz and I had gotten to be so close, we'd always be friends no matter what I decided. I watched her as she bent over to tie her shoes, her pale gold hair fanning out around her face. I was thinking how pretty she was and how I liked her better than any friend I'd ever had . . . except Tom.

"You're sure quiet today, Meg. What's the matter? Got your period?"

"No, but I feel rotten."

"What's the trouble?" Liz asked as she finished tying her shoes and straightened up to look me square in the eye.

"Well, I was just wondering about you being Pris's campaign manager."

"Look, I keep telling you not to worry about Pris and Beeb. They were just hanging out together. He didn't really like her, I swear."

"That's not what I meant. Why would you want her to go to the governor's conference?"

Liz shot me a look that made me feel I was crazy. "Why, Megan, she's a friend of ours."

"She's no friend of mine, and didn't you once tell me you thought she was manipulative and brash?"

"Hey, maybe she is, but you don't think I'd vote for someone I didn't even know." Liz was studying my face, and I guess my conflict showed. "You're part of the group now too, Megan. The kids've all really accepted you."

"You don't know how glad I am that they have, and I know you're the one that really made it happen for me. I mean, I really have fun with you, and Mickey . . . and now with Beeb. . . ."

"So what's the problem?" I was glad Liz hadn't made a move to go out on the floor. I knew we had to thrash this out, as much as I dreaded it. "You know, you're the first person we've taken in since . . . gee, I guess since Mickey moved here in fifth grade. I don't know why. Maybe we never thought about it.

But I liked you right away. Remember that day after 'Megan's Beat' came out for the first time—"

"Liz, this is really serious." I took a deep breath and said, "It's definite now. Tom's going to run against Pris."

"Oh, damn!" She touched my shoulder. "Gee, Megan, that's really going to make it tough for you, isn't it? I know you're going to feel terrible, since you and Tom've lived out there so close and every thing, but I'll bet he'll understand. I mean, he knows you're a Hi Gal and dating Beeb and everything."

"No, he won't. He asked me to be his campaign manager."

"His campaign manager? Why, you can't do that!"

"Why not?"

"Well, Megan, it's pretty obvious, isn't it? I mean the club always stays tight. We work as a unit. Every body expects that. I mean, how would it look?" Liz must have realized she was beginning to get my back up, because her tone changed. "I'm sorry, Megan, I really am, but Tom'll get over it. I mean, you're in our crowd now, and I think he understands that." She gave me a really straight look. "I've just always as sumed you wanted to be, even though you and Pris aren't ever going to be best friends or anything. I mean, we all like some more than others, but you understand Hi Gals just can't work against each other."

"I don't want to work against *you*, Liz. I really like you, but Tom and I have always known each other, and I went to school with all the kids on my bus, like you did with Mickey and Mike and . . . Pris. I've even told Tom I wouldn't be his campaign manager, but . . . he's like . . . family. You just don't know how torn up I am about this."

We got out on the floor, but we couldn't get together. I think it was because we didn't look at each other.

I just thought my heart would break. I'd been watching her and wishing she could be my friend for such a long time, and the thought of being a cheerleader with her was just like a dream. Besides that I really liked her. She was someone I could tell secrets to and laugh with. I just couldn't understand how she could be so dense about wanting me to betray Tom. Betray? Is that what I would be doing? Oh, I just wanted to die.

Just a few days earlier I had been looking forward to the hayride so much. Now I was all mixed up about it. Sometimes I thought we might still have fun, and other times I thought Daddy's horses were going to be pulling a time bomb along those roads. Finally I decided I was going to concentrate on having a good time. Any more decisions could wait until after the hayride.

I don't know how I got through the week. Friday night was slower coming than Christmas. I'd prayed it wouldn't rain, and it didn't. Rain would have spoiled everyone's fun because it had turned into quite a party. Since so many kids' parents had to drive them out to the farm, Mother said it was a waste of gas for them to make two trips, so she invited them to stay and help with the bonfire. Bill Arnold said it had been a month of Sundays since he'd sat around a campfire, so he and Ethel said they'd come too. That meant Tom hadn't told them about our fight. Ethel would have been on my case if he had. A few weeks back she'd gone to a revival and got to be a born-again Christian. Now she's worse than she used to be. If she starts preaching at my party, I'll go up in the woods to live in the log cabin.

Tom was still going to drive. I'd broken our silence long enough to ask him that, and he had said, "Sure. *I* keep my promises." Now what did he mean by that? I hadn't promised him a thing!

Even Mother thought Beeb looked like a dream when he arrived, wearing a white turtleneck sweater under his letter sweater with his athletic jacket thrown around his shoulders. In the winter all the athletes wear crimson jackets trimmed with white leather. Mike had only his jacket, but maybe Beeb thought it'd get cold on the ride. When I could avoid Tom's dirty looks, I was so proud of Beeb, I could hardly keep my feet on the ground.

Everyone made a big deal about finding a spot in the hay. Somebody pushed Bill Brannon clear off the wagon, but he didn't get hurt. Finally they all stopped scuffling, and Daddy and Tom went over the route we were supposed to follow about a hundred times. Pris said in a whisper loud enough for everyone to hear, "Some leader!" but everyone else seemed willing to forget about the conference. We were off.

At least for the night Liz was treating me like nothing had ever happened, and she got everybody to singing. We must have sung every fight song known and we sang our school song about a trillion times. Mickey was crazy about the big old Percherons, so she insisted we sing a song to them. I don't think Daddy would have been very pleased to hear us sing "The Ole Gray Mare" to his prize-winning team, but we couldn't think of anything else. Even Tom seemed to get a kick out of that song. Once at Heckathorne I had made up some funny lyrics to songs from "Oklahoma," and Tom and I had put on a skit that brought the house down. When we got together with Tim and those kids, we always sang it. But I knew better than to ask Tom now. He'd probably just snarl and embarrass me in front of Liz and Beeb and everyone. Then someone pointed out there was this beautiful full moon, so we sang "Shine On Harvest Moon." I decided not to worry anymore. Everything just seemed to be going perfect, even Pris was behaving herself. I guessed she wanted to make a good impression on Bud, since it was their first date.

It began to get colder, and I must have started to shiver, because Beeb put his arm around me and said, "Is that better?"

"Much," I said while my heartbeat speeded up.

He pulled me over closer to him, and I put my head on his shoulder, but I felt funny with all those other kids there. At least Tom had to watch the horses. But then I realized everyone had suddenly gotten very quiet. I looked over Beeb's shoulder just once. He put his other arm around me and moved his cheek against mine. I'd never felt so good in my life. We lay back in the hay, and he propped himself up on one elbow and just looked at me for a long time.

One side of me was so happy, I thought I'd blow apart, but every time I opened my eyes, I had to look at Tom's back. He usually slouches all over the place, but he was sitting up there like a soldier. I looked back at Beeb and tried not to think about it.

"Megan, you're so pretty," he whispered and then he just brushed my lips with his. I *really* liked that. Then he kissed me all the way. It was wonderful! So we just kept it up. I squeezed my eyes shut real tight, and I couldn't even see Tom.

Long before I was ready, Tom turned around and said, "I can see the bonfire." I don't know if he saw us or not. It was pretty dark.

"Good, it's getting cold," I said to Tom, just to keep up appearances. I didn't really mean it.

Beeb took off his sweater and said, "Why don't you wear this?"

When we all piled off the hayrack, everyone said they needed the hot cider to get warm, but I didn't. All wrapped up in Beeb's letter sweater, I had never been so toasty in my life.

Tom took charge of roasting hot dogs and tending the fire. I didn't think much about him until I heard

Pris yell, "You burned mine! That's not fit to eat!" She was right. Her hot dog was *black*. I glanced at Tom, and for a moment we both forgot we were feuding, and grinned at each other. I'm still not sure it was an accident like he told Pris.

After we had eaten everything in sight, we sang some more songs. Liz made Mother and Daddy sing "Danny Boy," and at the end when Daddy took Mother's hands and sang the last chorus to her, I wasn't even embarrassed. After all Beeb was holding mine. They'd let Lizzie come to the bonfire, and she showed off something fierce. At first she clung on to Tom, but in a little while she was sitting on every boy's lap. When she came over to us, I just knew what she would do and she *did*.

"Megan, where did you get that sweater? It's too big for you."

"It's Beeb's," I said very softly.

"Well, you better give it back to him 'cause Mother says it's time for everyone to go home now."

"That's okay, Lizzie, she can keep it," said Beeb. "I think it really looks good on her, don't you?"

I couldn't believe it! Daddy was so wrong. I'd *never* tire of him. Things were going so well, I just couldn't understand why the governor had to think up a stupid ole conference to mess everything up.

When people were getting in their cars and telling Mother and Daddy how much fun they'd had, in my mind I was writing an item for my column that would never be printed:

Under a harvest moon, in a pile of sweet-smelling hay, Megan Morgan had her first kiss, and it was terrific! The letter sweater she was wearing after the hayride indicates Beeb Barber thought it was pretty terrific too. The kids who live in Sagamon had such a good time at the Morgan farm, I hear they're planning another party where all the kids from surrounding farms will be invited. Looks like a new era has begun.

I watched Tom get into the car with his folks. No one even told him good-bye. That woke me up fast. It would never happen. Why was I kidding myself?

Mickey was the last to leave. She came running up to me and said, "Megan, I just love the farm. Gee, you're lucky."

There were those words again. "Thanks, Mickey," was all I said. It had gotten too complicated to try to explain to anybody.

I'd promised myself I'd decide what I was going to do after the hayride. Well, mulling everything over just about ruined my weekend. Wednesday the candidates had to announce who their campaign managers were going to be. I knew Tom hadn't picked anyone else. Even though no one on the bus was talking to me, I would have heard them talking about it to each other if he had. And, of course, I couldn't forget that Liz and the other Hi Gals expected me to back Pris, no matter what.

Saturday morning Ethel called Mother, so I knew Tom had told his folks I'd refused to be his campaign manager. They probably had noticed we weren't very friendly at the bonfire and had made him tell them why. Ethel preached to Mother about the Christian thing for me to do. I heard Mother say she thought kids had to work things like this out among themselves, that it was part of growing up, but I could tell Ethel didn't agree.

In the afternoon I went down to the pasture and whistled for Prince. Without a saddle it wasn't quite so easy, but I finally got on his back and we wandered around for a while. He just went wherever he felt like. After a time he stopped down by the bridge, and I lay down on him like he was a mattress. This whole business was just wearing me out. I couldn't even enjoy dreaming about Beeb, but I did wear his sweater all day. Daddy had almost reached the bridge before I heard him, even though that ole Allis makes a heck of a noise. He stopped the tractor on the bridge.

"Strange place to be taking your rest, Megan," Daddy said. He leaned back, stretching his shoulder muscles. I guess he needed a rest too. "Anything special tire you out today?"

I didn't start out planning to talk to him about the mess I was in with Tom, but without hardly knowing what I was doing, I just spilled it all out. You know, sometimes parents just surprise you. Now, after I got started, I fully expected him to yell at me and take on something terrible about me being loyal to my own, not changing my stripes, and all that stuff.

But the funniest thing happened. He didn't at all. He let me talk, then he said, "Sometimes it's hard to make decisions. I've been buffaloed more than once myself. But Lucy's always telling me you're a born leader."

"You just think I'm bossy."

"Well, you weren't exactly what I was expecting in a little girl, I reckon." He took off his cap and smoothed back his hair. "But, heck, I should've been prepared for that after fifteen years of living with your mother." He chuckled, put his cap back on, and then looked at me very seriously, just the way he does at Bill Arnold or Mother.

"Your mother knows more about things like this than I do. So, she's probably got you pegged right. If that's true, I guess when you know what's right, you'll be doing it."

I should have known his treating me like a grownup couldn't last. Before what he had said hardly had time to sink in, he asked, "You fed the chickens yet?"

"Nope."

"Hop on, then. You better get to it."

He fired up the ole Allis, and we clanged on up the hill. In Daddy's book even born leaders do their chores.

Sixteen

* * * * * * * * * * * * *

Monday morning I didn't have any trouble deciding what to wear to school. Since I sure couldn't go over to Tom's on Sunday like I usually did, I had gone through my whole closet and decided Beeb's sweater would go with everything I owned except maybe the plaid skirt with the bright red stripe. I never did like that skirt anyway. I couldn't figure out how many times I should wear the sweater in one week. If I wore it every day, people would think I was showing off; but if I didn't, Beeb might think I didn't appreciate it. Liz only wears Mike's about once a week, but she's had it for a long time. I thought if she called, I'd ask her opinion, but she didn't. I didn't know why I hadn't called her—well, yes, I really did. I felt awkward about our conversation before cheerleading practice, and I still wasn't sure what I was going to do. It was easier to think about the sweater, so I decided to wear it on Monday and Friday the first week, and to Hi Gal meeting on Wednesday night—to Hi Gal meeting for sure! Of course that was assuming I had the sweater for a week and went to the meeting at all.

I had to wear my coat to walk out to meet the bus, and we never took our coats off just to ride into town, so none of the farm kids knew I had it on. That was as frustrating as having to wear gloves over a big ole diamond ring. But even if they couldn't see it, the sweater felt kind of like a shield against their coldness. Tom wouldn't even look at me all the way to town.

Liz stopped by my desk before biology and said, "Hey, Megan, we'll have to practice during study period today because at lunch we've got to come up with Pris's campaign slogan to put on posters and in 'Megan's Beat.'"

I couldn't believe it! After I had told her how I felt in the gym Friday, how could she just assume I was going to go along with her gang . . . *our* gang? I still hadn't decided what I was going to do. I did know I wasn't going to help elect Pris. That I knew for sure!

"I'll talk to you later," I said, because Mrs. Horner was starting class. She passed out slides and told us to pair off with the person across the aisle on our right to look through the microscopes. That meant Pris was supposed to share with Suzy Lane, but she just turned her back on Suzy without saying a word and went over to look through Liz and Mickey's microscope. Mrs. Horner didn't even seem to notice. For just a moment Suzy looked surprised and kind of hurt, then she just shrugged her shoulders and started fiddling with her slide.

The campaign managers were going to be announced Wednesday. I knew time was running out and I had to take a stand. I could take my column to Mr. Finley at lunch and avoid the Hi Gals, but I'd have to go to cheerleading practice seventh period. I had to come up with a plan for action, and I just wasn't ready yet. *Why did this ever have to happen?* I asked myself for about the millionth time.

Before English class I waited outside the door because I wanted to talk to Beeb. I decided I might as well know just how much I had to lose, even though my heart hurt just thinking about it. Mr. Wills kept looking at his watch. Sometimes teachers think kids have nothing on their minds except their stupid classes.

When Beeb and Mike showed up, I grabbed Beeb's arm. "Wait a minute, I've got to talk to you."

He grinned, but when he looked in and Mr. Wills gave us a dirty look, his face got red.

"Can you find a way to come out to the farm tonight? I really need to talk to you."

Before he could answer, Mr. Wills appeared at the door and said, "Well, I hate to interrupt you two lovebirds, but if you wouldn't mind joining us, the rest of the class is ready to get started."

Beeb's face flashed like a stoplight. I wanted to strangle Mr. Wills, but Beeb ducked his head and hurried into class. I was so mad, I didn't hurry at all. As a matter of fact I gave him a dirty look and took my time getting to my seat.

After class Beeb was waiting for me down the hall from Wills's room, and he still seemed pretty embarrassed.

"I'd really like to come out tonight, Megan, but I can't. I promised Mike I'd help him build some contraption Liz wants to put Pris's campaign posters on."

Since he's shy, I guess I usually give Beeb more encouragement than I was able to muster right then, because he stopped and look at me quizzically. "But I'll call you. Is it something you can tell me on the phone?"

He put his hand on my shoulder, and the same old quivers went trotting down my spine, even though I was feeling miserable. Maybe I was going to be a sex maniac.

"Are you going to work for Pris?" I asked him.

"Hey, you're my girl, remember?" he said, and put his thumb under the edge of his sweater. "Don't look so sour. I'll just help Mike out. You know, the same things I'd do if any of the gang was running. You know I never did have a big thing for Pris."

I had my hair in two ponytails, and he pulled one like a lamp cord. "Come on, Meg, smile."

"Beeb, did you ever like anyone who wasn't a Hi Gal?"

"I only like one Hi Gal, even though sometimes she can get worried about nothing." He dropped his arm around my shoulders and started moving me down the hall. I knew he was in a hurry to get to basketball practice.

"Would you like me just as much if I weren't a Hi Gal?"

"What a dumb question. You are a Hi Gal." He looked puzzled. "What's the matter with you today? I don't care anything about that club. Those girls have been forming clubs since we were in first grade. They used to have one that met under the railroad trestle bridge, and they never would tell the guys what they did under there."

He was just like Liz and Mike. As far as he was concerned, the only people in the world were in his gang or on the opposing team. Suddenly I wanted to shake him hard and say, "Look at all these other kids going down the hall. They're not insects. They've got lives that count too."

But what I really said was "You better get to practice. Coach'll be on your tail, too, if you're late."

"Did you and Liz practice today? I want you to be good. It'll really be neat if you get to be a cheerleader. We'll get to see each other tons more."

"Liz and I can't seem to get our act together today. We're supposed to be practicing this period, but she had to make up a Latin test instead. I'm . ... not sure I'll be going out with her."

"Why not?" He looked as mixed up as I felt.

I hadn't planned on telling him—I mean, why close the shutters before you're even sure there's a storm?—but then I just blurted it out.

"Well, you must have heard that Tom Arnold's going to run against Pris for the governor's conference." I stopped, waiting for him to see the problem, but he just looked at me blankly. "You see, Tom's really a *good* friend of mine."

"Oh, I see." Beeb looked as if he were in pain. "Gee, Meg, that'll really make it tough for you with the Hi Gals, won't it? I mean, I can see why you'd just want to stay out of the whole thing, but we're all going to be roped into Pris's campaign because of Liz and Mike and everything." He gave me one of his sympathetic, sweet looks. "No wonder you're upset."

"Beeb, Tom asked me to be his campaign manager."

"His campaign manager? Oh, Megan, I wouldn't do that if I were you. I mean, the campaign'll only go on for a couple of weeks, and if you just sort of stay out of it, Pris and Liz might be kind of upset at first, but they'll get over it when cheerleading season starts and everybody gets caught up in how we're doing in our section. I mean we've got a strong team this year, but Pana's good and . . ."

I couldn't listen to him anymore. Suddenly I just wanted him to leave. "Listen, you're going to be late. Call me tonight, okay?"

He got about three steps down the hall and called back, "Meg, you're going to try out, aren't you?"

"Oh, sure," I said. "I'm not only going to try out, I'm going to make it! Wait and see."

I wasn't mad at Beeb, but I sure was disappointed. Still, how could I expect him to be any different?

hat's just the way he is, I'm beginning to find out.
 couldn't help but think that even though Tom
 asn't always out there leading the band, at least he
 d a mind of his own. Even when I could talk him
 to things, it always took some horse trading. He
 ever was a pushover. Betty Sue was like that too.
 ometimes her judgment was kind of awful, but she
 d spirit, and it was her own. All of a sudden I missed
 l those kids like I'd been on a long trip. Then I told
 yself that I was really being stupid. Think of the
 n I'd had with Liz, and how it felt when Beeb
 ssed me, and when basketball season started. . . .

 I guess I had put my head down when Beeb and I
 rted because the next thing I knew I ran smack
 to Suzy Lane, the girl in my biology class whose
 ter had split her pants. She was digging around in
 er locker and didn't see me coming.

 "Whoops! Gee, I'm sorry, Suzy. Guess I wasn't look-
 g where I was going. You okay?"

 "No, but who *could* be around this place?"

 Suzy lived in town and she seemed to have friends,
 t as far as I could tell, about all they did was show
 p for classes. They were sort of like a non-group.
 hey weren't smart like those kids Kitty wanted to
 in around with, and they weren't popular like the
 i Gals. They didn't even seem to have anything like
 ; or 4-H like the country kids did. No wonder she
 d a bad attitude.

 "What's the matter with you?" Suzy asked. "You
 ok terrible. Beeb got a new girl or something?"

189

"No, not yet. I'm just feeling low."

"What've you got to be upset about, I'd like know? You sail in here, Mary Milkmaiden straigh off the farm, and before any of us even find our hom rooms you've got a column in the paper, a bigshot fe a boyfriend, and you break the tightest clique : school. Yeah, Megan, cry your eyes out. You've real got a problem, all right."

"If it hadn't been for 'Megan's Beat,' none of th rest of it probably would have happened."

"So who cares? Before you none of the country ki ever did *anything* around here, believe me. My sist graduated last year, and she wasn't in the hotsh crowd either, but like she used to tell me, 'I ain't c the bottom of the ladder. There's still the bus kid It's like you broke the color barrier or somethin I even heard you've got a good chance to be a chee leader."

As we were talking I suddenly realized that Su: and people like her formed a huge, unaffiliated votir bloc. "Suzy, who're you going to vote for to go to th governor's conference?"

"I don't even know who's running. None of n friends, you can bet on that."

"From our class it's probably going to be To Arnold and Pris White."

"Look, Megan, you're okay, and Liz Ray's not : bad sometimes, but your friend Pris is the lowes She doesn't care how she makes anyone feel." Unt Suzy said that, I had forgotten about Pris snubbir her in biology this morning. Probably there were lots of kids around she'd alienated that way.

"Oh, I know she'll win, but she's such a snot," Suzy went on.

"But you'd vote for her?" I asked.

"What difference does it make? You know how it is around here. In every class a few kids always expect to be the leader, and they are, you know what I mean? Hey, Megan, why aren't you running? We'd vote for you."

I wasn't about to admit to Suzy Lane or anybody else how I'd felt when Tom said the bus kids would have nominated me if I hadn't been so involved with Pris and the Hi Gals. I hadn't even admitted to myself how much I'd like to go to that conference. Getting people involved the way the governor was promoting in the conference was really my kind of thing. But my old friends hadn't picked me. They'd picked Tom and put me in front of a firing squad. So I just said, "I've got to go, Suzy, but let's talk about this some more. Maybe in biology tomorrow, okay?"

I had seen Trisha Ponds go past, and I took off after her, weaving my way through the crowd like a swivel-hipped quarterback. "Hey, Trisha," I yelled, just as she had started into a classroom. She was in my Latin class, but I'd never said a word to her, so I really had to pull something out of the air to start up a conversation. "I got a letter from Kitty, and she told me to be sure and say hello to you," I said, feeling like a phony.

"Kitty?" Trisha squinted at me as if she weren't even sure who I was.

"You remember Cancan Kitty?" Now why did I say that? Kitty would kill me if she knew. "She was that real smart girl from Chicago who only went here for a few weeks and then went back to go to that school for real intelligent kids."

"Oh, her. Well, sure . . . tell her hi."

"Listen, Trisha, I was just wondering, since we're talking and everything, who are you going to vote for to go to the leadership conference in Springfield?"

"I didn't even know about it. My friends and I aren't interested in politics."

"You know, Trisha, that's just what's wrong with this country. Smart people like you and your friends should get involved, then we wouldn't have crooks like Nixon getting elected."

"Intellectuals can't get elected. Look at Stevenson."

Daddy says that man thought farmers spoke Swahili, but I didn't tell her that. "Well, maybe the kids who go to this leadership conference can begin to do something about that. If I come back to ask for your ideas when the campaign gets started, would you think about doing some work?" She frowned. "Maybe just with your group?"

"Well, maybe with my friends."

Give me a break! This school is incredible. Every group has their own Berlin Wall. "Okay. Don't forget. I'll talk to you again."

"Who are you backing?" Trisha asked as I darted away.

"I'll tell you all about it on Wednesday," I called back over my shoulder, heading for my locker.

When I opened my locker door, I caught a glimpse of my face in the mirror I'd taped on the back before I'd started going with Beeb so I could always check to see how I looked before I went to English class. I steadied the door and took a good look. Remarkable! I knew if somebody could photograph me from the inside, I'd look like last year's crabapples. I'd been such a child when I put up that mirror. Writing "Megan's Beat" and everything that followed had made me grow up fast. I'd gotten enough responsibility to give me indigestion.

Mickey was supposed to be making up the Latin test with Liz, but she must have been held up someplace, because she came past my locker like the Road Runner. When she caught me gazing into my mirror, she skidded to a stop.

"Hey, Meg, wouldn't you know Mr. Miller would schedule that stupid Latin make-up for when we should be practicing? We can get in some extra time after school on Wednesday before Hi Gals meeting, I guess. I know we have to work on Pris's posters during the meeting, but we really need to practice that routine where we do the splits at the end. Too bad Liz can't do flips. That would really jazz up our act. There's just too much going on right now."

I took a deep breath and said, "Mickey, I'm not going to work on Pris's campaign."

"What? Well, why not?" She didn't have to look at me as if I'd said I was going to shoot the principal.

"Because . . . because I don't want her to win."

"Pris'll kill you!" She actually looked scared. "Oh, Meg, don't make Pris of all people mad before cheerleader tryouts. I mean she can really sway the votes. She could ruin our chances."

"Cheerleaders should be picked by how good they are, not how much Pris White likes them," I said and thought, *Yeah, and no one should steal hubcaps or beat their kids either.*

"But you *know* that's not the way it works. Listen, I've got to go. I'm already late, but we've got to talk about this." She turned back and asked, "Who do you want to win, for Pete's sake?"

"Tom Arnold." Mickey must really be out of it.

"Oh, him."

Mickey had so much pep and was so much fun. I'd just die if we weren't friends after this was all over. We would be! I just wouldn't let the conference election wreck everything, but right now I had other things to do. I slammed my locker, and with a renewed surge of determination headed toward the gym. I had a lot to do before this day was over.

I cut study hall and went to see Miss Robinson, who sponsors the cheerleaders.

"Hi, Megan," she said, and waved me to a seat

across from her desk. "How're your muscles? Still sore?"

They don't hurt as much as my head, I wanted to tell her. What I did say was "Miss Robinson, do you think there's any chance the cheerleaders could practice during lunch or study, rather than after school?"

"Well, I don't know. I'd just never thought about it. I guess it doesn't matter so much when, just as long as they get the time in. Of course before a tournament or when they are breaking in new routines . . ."

"But that wouldn't be very often, right?"

"No, I guess not. What's the matter? Are you and Liz and Mickey running into some difficulty?"

"No, ma'am," I kind of looked out the window, in case my voice cracked or tears came in my eyes or anything. "I might not be going out with those kids after all."

"You're not quitting Hi Gals or anything like that, are you, Megan?" She sure was looking hard at my face, like she was trying to read it or something.

"No, I'm not!" I said that louder than I intended to. "But I just might not be as . . . uh, active for a while. I don't really know yet." I knew I was sounding like an idiot.

"Oh, I see. Well, who are you going to be trying out with, Megan? I should know so that I can change the roster."

"Well, I can't really tell you today. You see the person I'm going out with doesn't know it yet, but as soon as everything is all squared away, I'll come back. Okay?"

"Oh, I see . . . sure. You come on back when you get it worked out." I could feel her watching me with that funny look on her face, even after I beat it out of her office.

I read my history again on the bus going home. I kept wishing Mr. Blair could see me. He wouldn't have to know that I never did turn the page.

When Henry stopped at the farm, I waited until I had got to the door, so everybody would hear, and then I said, "Tom, I want to talk to you." I've never seen him move so fast, and I've never heard the bus so quiet.

When we got to the creek bridge, I sat down and said, "Okay, here's the deal. I'll be your bloody campaign manager, but—"

"Whoopie!" He did three cartwheels in a row and almost fell in the creek.

"Save your energy because you're going to need it. I'm going to be your campaign manager *and* you're going out for cheerleading with me!"

"Oh, no I'm not! Now Megan, that—"

"It's not for sissies. How could anyone who is chosen to sit down and talk politics with the governor be considered a sissy?"

"Well, yeah, but, no . . . I can't get out there and jump around—"

"Do you want me to get you elected or not?"

"That's not a fair trade."

"I learned horse tradin' from a master. When I think of some of the deals you've made with me . . . Believe me, Tom, this one's costing me more than you know."

"If you mean choosing between those snobby Hi Gals and the kids who've been your friends all your life, I don't think that's such a big deal."

"I'm not giving up on my friends from town either! Oh, look, I know Pris is no prize, but I like Liz and Mickey a lot. What we have to do is work on everybody's attitude."

"Look, Megan, I don't even know what you're talking about. I just want to go to the governor's conference."

"Then teach me to do a flip."

"You know, you're the most contrary, stubbornest, hardheadedest girl I've ever known." He had a hand on each hip and was leaning over me and preaching just like Ethel. "Well, stand up. You can't very well do a flip sitting down. Hey, this is crazy. Even if we were to make it, cheerleaders practice after school, I bet."

"I think I fixed that."

"Pretty sure of yourself, weren't you? You're really cocky, you know that, Megan?"

"A shrinking violet wouldn't get anyone with a face like yours elected to anything. I've also started working on the fringe vote. What we'll do is put one kid on each bus in charge of bringing in votes from his bus. We'll have to write an editorial kind of thing saying it was time the bus kids banded together, then get flyers passed out. In assemblies we'll stress what a wide constituency you represent and what an all-around guy you are."

"You're crazy. All I belong to is FFA."

"But by that time you'll be trying out for cheer-leader. We'll make a big thing out of you being the first boy to ever do it."

Tom grabbed his head. "Cripes! They *will* say I'm a sissy! I know they will!"

"In your campaign speeches you'll talk about how Rudy's going to be a grand champion. Sissies don't raise bulls! Now how do I stand when I want to flip backwards?"

"Megan, I just don't know about this."

Mother was right, you just have to treat 'em like babies. "Look, Tom, you're an outstanding tumbler. Everybody's going to think you're terrific. I bet next year more guys will try out than girls. Now, what do I do?"

He held my back and showed me how to do three flips in a row. Then I drove him home.

Mother was just getting off the phone when I pitched my history book onto the kitchen table. "Megan, that was Betty Sue's mother. She's real worried about her. Says Betty Sue's getting out of hand. You know anything about that?"

"She might be starting to hang around with a bad crowd."

"Her mother wondered if you'd come over for supper Thursday night. She said you hadn't been around much since school started. Will you go?"

"Sure." I was going to need Betty Sue to work on the campaign. She wasn't bad at drawing.

"What were the tricks you and Tom were doing down on the bridge?" Mother asked.

"I . . . I'm going to be Tom's campaign manager." I put my head down on the table and cried like a baby.

Mother patted my shoulder and said, "Oh, honey, I'm so sorry everything has to be so hard for you. How are you going to use those tricks to get Tom elected?"

I threw my head back. Crying didn't help at all. "That's going to get us chosen as cheerleaders. We made a deal."

"You two always have."

"Well, if he thought I was going to give up the whole basketball season and bus trips with the team for his sake, he's crazy. I don't plan on being a martyr." I marched outside to feed those stupid chickens.

I went to my room right after supper. When Lizzie came up to see what I was doing, I said, "I've got a present for you, Lizzie."

When I took the box with my Brenda Starr paper dolls off the shelf, you would have thought I'd given her the Hope diamond, the way she carried on.

"To keep forever?"

"Sure. I won't be playing with them anymore."

She gave me such a big hug, she dropped the box

and spilled them all over the floor. She's such a klutz. We were down on our knees picking them up, and she asked, "Megan, why're you wearing that boy's sweater over your pajamas? That looks silly."

I just told her I was cold. You can't explain anything to a five-year-old.

When Mother came upstairs to bed, she stood in the door of my room to say good night. I was practicing splits. Sometimes we talk in shorthand. She didn't make me spell out all the questions I had floating around in my head, or how much they hurt. I didn't have to tell her I was making elaborate plans to strangle Tom Arnold . . . slowly, after this was all over.

She just said, "You're getting better. You're almost all the way to the floor."

I got into a more comfortable position and said, "I'll have it down pat by tryouts. I think we've got a good chance. You know a boy-and-girl combination might be unique enough to win, since Sagamon never had a boy cheerleader."

Mother smiled. "Sure. Tom's so limber, I bet he'll be good, and you can practice with him on weekends. And it would seem to me that if Mickey and Liz win, too, you'll have to work together."

"I'm kind of counting on that." I swallowed hard and said, "Mother, I guess I'll probably take my lunch and eat outside tomorrow. Do you have anything hot to put in a Thermos?" Crying just wasn't going to help a bit.

"Sure, I'll give you some beef stew."

"It'll probably take me a few days to get Tom and Tim to eat in the lunchroom again, and we've got lots of work to do."

She just stood there, leaning against the doorframe. I guess she knew it wouldn't do any good to talk about sometimes having to do what you knew was right, even when it hurt a lot. She came over to kiss me good night and squeezed me extra hard.

"Good night, Megan. I'm glad you're a fighter. I know these have been very difficult decisions." As she closed the door she said, "I'm proud of you."

Beeb, Liz, all of them, were going to have to make some difficult decisions, I thought after she left. I was really miserable, but then I thought, *Priscilla White writing laws for us? Maybe even getting to be a senator or the governor? Well, we'll see about that!* I pulled out my notebook and started writing my next column. After all, I was still Megan ****** Starr ****** Reporter:

> *I've asked Mr. Finley to give Priscilla White's campaign manager equal time because for the next two weeks I will be devoting "Megan's Beat" to telling SHS students why I think Tom Arnold should be our candidate for the Governor's Leadership Conference.*